Echoes of

Legends

Written by: William Henry Belmont

Edited by: Luna

This book is a work of fiction. Names, characters, places, and events are the product of the author's imagination. Any resemblance to actual persons, living or dead, or to actual events is purely coincidental.

ISBN: 979-8-218-92201-6

First edition

Printed in the United States of America

Content

Part 1: The Sacred Princess

William Henry Belmont

Our story begins as stories often do, with a young a beautiful heroine; but as it happens, she does not know she is a heroine yet. At this time, she still thinks she is but a simple woman from a humble family.

Isabella Galeon is a striking young woman in her early 20s, possessing an aura of both strength and grace. Her long, dark brown wavy hair that cascades down her back, with bangs framing her face, adding a touch of wild elegance. Her skin, a warm bronze reminiscent of the ancient native gods, speaks to her rich heritage. Isabella is not just beautiful; her expressive brown eyes hold a depth of knowledge and determination that reflects her dual life as a historian and a fighter. Standing at medium height, her toned physique is a testament to her rigorous training in the ring. Isabella's beauty is both classic and fierce, capturing the essence of her powerful and complex character.

One day, Isabella was, as she often is, deep in her element, navigating the dimly lit aisles of an old library in a dusty border town. The scent of aged paper and the soft rustle of turning pages surround her as she meticulously searches for resources for her studies. However, despite hours of searching, she finds nothing new, only familiar texts she has already pored over countless times. Frustration begins to set in, as Isabella knows that her research hinges on uncovering fresh, untapped sources of historical knowledge.

Disheartened but undeterred, Isabella steps out into the vibrant streets of her town. The late afternoon sun casts long shadows, and the lively sounds of the town fill the air. As she walks, lost in thought, a mysterious vendor catches her eye. The man, seemingly out of place among the usual market stalls, stands by a small table loaded with various curiosities. His eyes lock onto hers, and he gestures for her to come closer. Intrigued, Isabella approaches him.

William Henry Belmont

With a knowing smile, the vendor reaches under the table and pulls out a worn leather book. The book looks ancient, its cover weathered and cracked, with faded gold lettering that she can barely make out. Isabella's heart quickens. There's something almost magnetic about the book, a sense that it holds secrets long forgotten. The vendor hands it to her without a word, his eyes twinkling with a hint of mystery. As Isabella carefully takes the book into her hands, she feels a strange sensation, as if history itself is whispering to her from its pages.

This unexpected encounter marks the beginning of a journey that will blur the lines between the past and the present, history and myth, reality and the unknown.

As Isabella's fingers brushed the worn leather cover of the book to open it, a sudden, electric jolt surged through her body. The busy market scene around her dissolved, replaced by a desolate, post-apocalyptic landscape. The vibrant buildings and streets from the border town now laid in ruins before her, the remnants of once-grand structures now lying in disarray. Amidst the devastation, a dark figure emerged from the shadows, absorbing the last vestiges of light from the air. The figure clutched a staff, Isabella could not make who the mysterious person was, it was as if shadows covered its face permanently.

As the dark figure took a few steps towards her, Isabella's breath caught in her throat. Her heart pounded in her chest, each beat echoing in her ears like a drum. A chill ran down her spine. The air around her seemed to grow colder, as if the figure was draining the warmth from the very air. When the figure's eyes, glowing like crimson, locked onto hers, a wave of dread washed over her. Isabella's mouth went dry, and her hands trembled. The suffocation presence of the figure pressed on her like an invisible force; Isabella could not help but to feel a primal fear clawing at her.

Isabella's vision shifted; she was no longer standing in her town in ruins. She did not know where she was. She was standing in a dim lit place, the walls were made of massive rough stone blocks, giving a sense of ancient grandeur. She saw another figure, clothed in shining armor, standing resolutely amidst the stone chamber. The armor emitted a faint, ethereal glow, and as the figure removed its helmet, she recognized the face of Sir Percival, the fearless knight of the round table. "How could this possibly be" Isabella thought to herself. Sir Persival was a mythical character of stories she read, but not a real person. Percival's eyes, filled with profound wisdom and urgency, locked onto hers.

"Isabella, descendant of my bloodline," Sir Percival's voice resonated in throughout the massive chamber. "The time of great peril is upon us. A darkness, born of Morgana's legacy, threatens to engulf the world. Luca, the wielder of the Staff of Death, must be stopped."

With a sweeping gesture, Sir Percival revealed a vision of a towering stone pyramid, its steep steps rising towards the heavens, where the serpent god sleeps, a relic of an ancient civilization that once ruled the jungles. "Within the heart of the temple lies my axe, forged from the metals of the earth and imbued with elemental power. It is the only weapon capable of defeating Luca. You must journey to the pyramid, claim the axe, and unite with the other descendants of my companions. The fate of the world rests on your shoulders."

As the vision dissipated, Isabella found herself back in the market, the worn leather book still clutched in her hand. The vendor's voice cut through her daze. "Ah, señorita, I see you've found what you were looking for." A puzzled Isabella walked away from the vender and sat on the library's steps. The book, now weighted with an extraordinary significance, felt weighty in her grasp. Isabella knew her journey had only just begun, and with it, the destiny of many hung in the balance.

Isabella sat in her dimly lit study, the worn leather book resting on the table before her. Her mind buzzed with the remnants of the vision she had experienced, the image of Percival and the cryptic message still vivid in her thoughts. Doubt fell at her. "Can magic be real?" she wondered aloud. "Are the legends true?"

As a historian, Isabella had always relied on facts and evidence, but the vision had shaken her understanding of reality. Determined to find answers, she probed into her extensive collection of books and texts, poring over ancient manuscripts and obscure records. Her fingers traced the yellowed and torn pages as she searched for any hint of the extraordinary claims she had witnessed. Many nights all Isabella could hear was the flutter sound of pages turning in her study.

After days of relentless research, Isabella stumbled upon a surprising revelation. According to a long-forgotten chronicle, King Arthur and his legendary Knights of the Round Table had anticipated that even after their victory over Morgana, the threat would not be entirely eradicated. They knew that a descendant of Morgana would rise to challenge the world once more. To safeguard their sacred weapons and the legacy of their battle against darkness, the knights devised a cunning plan.

King Arthur and his knights took advantage of the old country Empire's colonialist expansion to conceal their powerful weapons in various locations around the globe. These sacred weapons were hidden in distant lands, out of reach from any single adversary, ensuring their protection against future threats.

The chronicle continued, detailing how, in the final years of their lives, Arthur, Lancelot, Percival, and Merlin made their way to the New World. Their goal was to establish a new base far from the clutches of Morgana and the old country. They settled discreetly, blending into the fabric of the growing nation, and their bloodlines ultimately merged with the local populace. This is how the storied lineage of the Round Table had ended up in the new world, waiting for the day when their descendants would be called upon once more.

William Henry Belmont

As Isabella read the last lines, a shiver ran down her spine. She never gave a second thought to her own last name, why would she. Finally at this moment it dawned on her, her last name Galeon hid in plain sight her linage, she was the decedent of the brave Knight Sir Percival Galois. The historical records had provided her with a framework that aligned with the vision she had received. The legends were not mere stories but encoded truths about a hidden legacy. Her skepticism began to fade, replaced by a profound sense of purpose. She realized that her journey was not just an academic pursuit but a crucial part of an ancient prophecy. The fate of the world, and perhaps her own destiny, was now intertwined with the echoes of history she had once thought were mere myth.

Armed with this newfound knowledge, Isabella resolved to follow the path outlined by Sir Percival. Understanding the gravity of the task ahead, she knew she needed to join forces with the descendants of the valiant knights. However, Sir

Percival had provided no further guidance beyond this vague direction. Determined to uncover the next steps, Isabella focused on the sole clue she had: the Pyramid of the ancient jungle civilization. She set her sights on this ancient site, hoping that it would lead her to the elusive axe mentioned in her vision. Along her journey, she could only hope to encounter further clues or information that would help her locate the other descendants she was meant to join.

On 21st day of the third month, Isabella had traveled and found herself amidst the ancient ruins of the ancient Peninsula, her heart racing with anticipation. The Pyramid stood before her, its towering presence casting long shadows in the afternoon sun. She had come to witness a rare celestial phenomenon, the moment when the shadows on the pyramid's steps align to form the plumed serpent, Kukulkan. According to legend, this event held deep mystical significance, a merging of celestial and earthly realms. If there was ever a time in which she could

William Henry Belmont

find knowledge about her vision, it would be this day.

As the shadows began to converge and the shape of the serpent materialized on the pyramid's surface, an old shaman emerged from the crowd. His weathered face, etched with lines of age and wisdom, was illuminated by the shifting light. He approached Isabella with a knowing gaze and spoke in a voice that seemed to carry the weight of centuries. "Return at night xch'ùupal," he advised. "During this sacred night, a hidden door will reveal itself to the true heir of the sacred artifact within the pyramid."

Isabella nodded, feeling a mixture of excitement and nervousness. As she was about to ask the shaman who he was, the shaman was no longer there, it appeared as if he had disappeared into the crown. She spent the hours leading up to dusk exploring the surrounding area, but her thoughts remained on the pyramid and the shaman's mysterious words. As the sun dipped below the horizon and darkness enveloped the landscape, she made her way back to the pyramid, its silhouette stark against the night sky.

Standing before the ancient structure, Isabella's eyes were drawn to a section of the pyramid that had previously been obscured in shadow. As she watched in awe, a secret door, camouflaged within the stonework, began to slowly open with a groaning creak. With a deep breath, she stepped through the threshold and entered the pyramid.

The air inside was cool, musty, and dense, shaded with the scent of ancient stone and earth. Isabella navigated through a narrow, winding passageway, her footsteps echoing off the walls. The passage was dimly lit by flickering torches that cast long, dancing shadows, and the walls were adorned with intricate carvings depicting scenes of native gods and celestial events. The passageway eventually opened into a grand, inner chamber; its ceiling vaulted high above. "This is it" Isabella said, "this is the chamber from my vision."

William Henry Belmont

In the center of the chamber stood an altar, its surface not adorned as the wall of the chamber were, the altar stood simple. Atop the altar rested a magnificent axe, its blade gleaming with an otherworldly light. The sight of the axe immediately reminded Isabella of the vision she had seen, affirming that she had found what she sought.

As she approached the altar, a rumbling sound shook the chamber, and the air grew thick with a palpable tension. The stone floor began to tremble, and from the shadows emerged a towering figure, Kukulkan, the feathered serpent god. His presence was imposing, a majestic transmutation of serpent and bird, with eyes that glowed like embers.

Kukulkan's voice, a deep and resonant echo, filled the chamber. "To claim the sacred axe, you must prove yourself worthy," he intoned. "Face the trials of your ancestors."

From the walls and floor, shadowy figures began to materialize, wraith-like apparitions of ancient warriors, their obsidian blades gleaming in the dim lighted chamber, echoes of a long-lost empire. Their forms shifting and merging like smoke. They advanced with menacing grace, their spectral weapons increasing their threat with each step. As Isabella's heart pounded in her chest, she braced herself for the test ahead.

The fierce and demanding battle began, a physical and mental trial that tested her strength, agility, and resolve. The shadowy figures attacked with a blend of precision and ferocity. Drawing on the fighting techniques Isabella had studied in ring; she began to fight back. She had had many opponents before but never faced danger in such a tangible form. Each strike and parry were a dance of survival, Isabella relying on her fighting skills and her determination to navigate the challenges.

As the trial progressed, Isabella felt a deep connection to the ancient warriors and the myths that had shaped her destiny. With every foe she vanquished, she grew more

William Henry Belmont

confident in her role as the true heir.
Finally, as the last shadowy figure
dissipated, Kukulkan's form began to re-
appear. Isabella stood victorious before the
plumed god. Once again, Kukulkan deep and
resonant voice filled the chamber, "You have
faced the trials of your ancestors with
courage and honor. Your strength and spirit
have proven you worthy. The sacred axe of
Sir Percival is yours. With it you shall
carry the legacy of whom came before you."
Isabella began to step towards the altar,
"Remember" said Kukulkan, "true power lies
not only in the might of the weapon but in
the heart of the bearer. Rise, true heir,
and fulfill your destiny." And with those
words, the feathered serpent god disappear
below the altar.

Exhausted but triumphant, Isabella
approached the altar once more, her hands
trembling slightly as she reached for the
sacred axe. As soon as her soft yet strong
hand touched the handle on the axe, once
again she felt an electric jolt running down

her spine, and she found herself immersed in a new vision.

Sir Percival appeared once more, his ethereal form standing before her in a timeless, otherworldly realm. His eyes, filled with a blend of pride and urgency, met hers.

"Congratulations, Isabella," Percival's voice resonated with warmth and approval. "You have proven yourself in the trial of Kukulkan and earned the sacred axe. Your strength and determination have brought you to this pivotal moment."

As Isabella held the axe in her hand, she felt an immense surge of power coursing through her veins. The weapon pulsed with vibrant energy, almost as if it was alive. Suddenly, the axe began to glow with a brilliant light, enveloping it in a radiant aura. The metal seemed to melt and reshape itself, transforming into a beautiful pendant.

The exquisite pendant, a delicate piece crafted from gold, with intricate designs etched into its surface. Adorned with touches of green emerald, glistening like droplets on a forest leaf, adding an elegant contrast to the gold. The center of the pendant held a small, perfectly cut emerald, surrounded by a series of tiny golden leaves that seemed to frame the stone like a precious gem in a royal crown. The design was both simple and majestic, a perfect representation of the powerful weapon it once was.

"Wear it," instructed Sir Percival, his voice echoing with a timeless authority. "The axe will manifest itself whenever you need it."

Isabella took the pendant and carefully placed it around her neck. The pendant settled elegantly against her skin, contrasting beautifully with her smooth complexion and long, flowing dark brown hair. The emerald pendant hung just above her collarbone, catching the light with every movement. The pendant felt warm against her skin, and as she wore it, she felt a deep connection to the weapon it had once been, and the destiny that lay before her.

Sir Percival paused, his gaze steady. "But your journey must continue at once. There is another heir you must seek. Travel to a vibrant city of the coastal west, where you will find Akira, the descendant of another Knight of the round table." Isabella stood in silence and deep in thought. "Find the heir of the Great Lancelot du Lac, together, you must unite and prepare for the trials that lie ahead. The fate of the world depends on it."

As the vision began to fade, Percival's image dissolved into the mist, leaving Isabella alone in the chamber with the pendent sitting around her neck and a renewed sense of purpose. The path was clear; her next destination was a vibrant city on the west coast, and her quest to find Akira was about to begin.

William Henry Belmont

Echoes of Legends

Part 2: The Windborne Champion

William Henry Belmont

After her adventure in the pyramid, Isabella now finds herself wandering the vibrant streets in the west coastal city, a historic district known for its rich cultural heritage. This city in particular has a blend of old-world charm and modern vitality, with traditional Eastern architecture standing side by side with contemporary storefronts. The streets are lined with old-fashioned shops offering everything from handcrafted pottery to exquisite raw fish dishes, and the aroma of incense and fresh food mingled in the air. Traditional Eastern lanterns and banners fluttered in the breeze, adding a festive touch to the bustling scene.

Feeling a mix of nervousness and determination, Isabella paused at a street corner, waiting for the vehicles to give her the opportunity to cross the road. As she scanned the surroundings, a street promoter seemed to appear out of nowhere, approaching her with an enthusiastic grin. Isabella couldn't help but think, "Where did this guy come from? I was just standing here alone…"

The promoter, dressed in bright, eye-catching attire, extended a glossy pamphlet towards her. "Ah, a tourist, I see! You must be looking for something to do while you're here, desu ne. Let me help you out!" Isabella took the pamphlet hesitantly, her preoccupation with her mission making her initially dismissive. "Thanks, but I'm actually here on a bit of a specific search," she said, trying to be polite but clearly distracted.

The promoter's eyes sparkled with excitement. "You might want to check out this event anyway. It's the National Eastern-style Championship, and it's happening right here in city. It's going to be quite a show!"

Isabella barely glanced at the pamphlet before putting it in her pocket and walking away, her mind still focused on finding Akira. After a few more streets, she felt a peculiar sensation, a sense that something was drawing her attention. She reached into her pocket and glanced down at the pamphlet in her hand, which had been folded and crumpled slightly from being tucked into her pocket. After opening it, Isabella's eyes widened as she scanned the information. The pamphlet featured bold, eye-catching graphics and details about the upcoming National Championship. It highlighted the event's significance and listed the fighters, including a prominent matchup between the reigning champion and the contender.

The champion was listed as Ryo DaCosta, a name that meant nothing to Isabella, she had never heard of that name before. But what caught her eye was the name of the contender: Akira Lake. Her heart skipped a beat. "Could this be the same Akira I am searching for?" she thought to herself. The pamphlet's bold print and colorful images made the event seem even more compelling. With a growing sense of curiosity and a hint of hope, Isabella decided to attend the championship.

Isabella attended the National Championship with a mix of anticipation and curiosity. The arena was filled with the buzz of excited spectators, the air filled with the scent of sweat and adrenaline. She found a seat with a good view of the fighting mat and watched as the fighters prepared for the main event: the match between the reigning champion, Ryo DaCosta, and the challenger, Akira Lake.

As the announcer introduced Akira, Isabella's eyes focused on him. Akira was of Eastern descent, his heritage apparent in his sharp, refined features. He was thin but well-toned, it was clear that Akira had been working out and training for years. His lean muscles rippling with every movement, exuding a blend of agility and strength. His hair was dark and messy, and his eyes were intense, reflecting a quiet confidence. He wore a simple white gi, his stance relaxed yet ready, embodying a disciplined warrior's spirit.

The match began with a flurry of calculated moves. Ryo, the more experienced fighter, displayed power and aggression, while Akira countered with speed and precision. The two fighters exchanged blows in a dance of martial prowess, each testing the other's limits. Akira moved with fluid grace, his strikes quick and precise, a testament to his rigorous training and focus. The crowd watched in awe as he countered Ryo's powerful attacks with deft footwork and rapid punches.

As the fight progressed, it became clear that Akira's strategy and agility were wearing down the champion. In a final, breathtaking move, Akira delivered a swift, spinning kick that landed squarely, sending Ryo to the mat. The crowd erupted in cheers as the referee raised Akira's hand, declaring him the new champion.

After the match, Isabella made her way through the crowds of fans and media, searching for Akira. As she finally spotted him, he looked up and their eyes met. To her surprise, he walked straight towards her, a look of recognition and surprise on his face. "It's you," Akira said, his voice laced with astonishment.

Isabella blinked, caught off guard. "Excuse me?" she asked, uncertain of his meaning.

Akira explained, "A few nights ago, I had a dream. In it, a beautiful woman approached me, and that woman… was you."

Intrigued and slightly unnerved, Isabella, almost blushing because of Akira's remark of "a beautiful woman" realized that their meeting was more than mere coincidence. She quickly recounted her own extraordinary experiences, from the vision of Sir Percival to the trial in the pyramid. She spoke of the ancient legacy they were both tied to and the mission they had to undertake together. As she described the visions, the history, and their magical nature, Akira listened intently, his expression, a mix of confusion and skepticism.

When she finished, Akira paused, still processing the surreal nature of what she had told him. "Visions and magic… it's a lot to take in," he admitted, his brow furrowed in thought. "But I can't ignore the dream I had, or the fact that you're here now, saying all this."

Curiosity piqued, still skeptical yet intrigued, Akira offered, "Why don't we go to my dojo? It's quieter there, and we can talk more. I need to understand all this better."

Isabella nodded, grateful for the chance to explain further. Together, they left the bustling arena, heading towards Akira's dojo to explore deeper into the mysteries that had brought them together.

As they arrived at Akira's dojo, a serene and traditional space adorned with calligraphy and wooden training equipment, Akira introduced Isabella to his sensei, an elderly man named Master Takashi. The sensei was a venerable figure, with a lean yet muscular build that hinted at a lifetime of martial arts mastery. His face was weathered with age, etched with lines of wisdom and experience. His eyes, sharp and penetrating, conveyed a deep understanding of the world and the martial arts. He wore a simple, elegant black robe with a white belt, symbolizing his mastery and years of dedication.

Master Takashi greeted Isabella with a polite nod before turning to Akira. "Akira," he said in a calm, authoritative voice, "I saw the tournament by broadcast, sorry I couldn't be there in person, I am too sickly to leave this dojo." Akira smiles at him, in recognition and respect to his Sensei. "There is something I must give you. It is the last lesson I was going to teach you." Said Master Takashi.

He walked to a corner of the dojo and retrieved a small, beautifully crafted blue chest decorated with intricate silver patterns. The chest seemed to glow softly under the dim light of the dojo, surely a relic from another time. Master Takashi carefully opened the chest and pulled out an ancient-looking scroll, rolled and tied with a thin red string. The parchment appeared fragile, its edges worn and faded with age.

He handed the scroll to Akira, who hesitated for a moment before taking it. As soon as Akira's fingers brushed against the scroll, a cold sensation shot through his head. His vision blurred, and he felt a powerful wind whip around him, swirling with the intensity of a hurricane. The dojo around him seemed to dissolve, and he stood puzzled, unable to comprehend what was happening.

When the wind subsided, Akira found himself in an entirely different place. He was inside an old temple, its ancient walls decorated with faded murals of mythical beasts and gods. The temple was dimly lit by paper lanterns, casting a warm, unearthly glow on the polished wooden floors. The architecture was grand yet solemn, with tall pillars and a high, ornate ceiling. The air was full of incense, creating an atmosphere of reverence and mysticism.

In front of Akira stood a man in shining armor, his presence commanding and noble, yet not completely corporal, more like a shadow of its former self. The knight's armor was intricately crafted, glinting in the soft light with a silver sheen. He wore a blue cape adorned with a golden lion, and his helmet, tucked under one arm, revealed a handsome, chiseled face with piercing blue eyes and shoulder-length blonde hair. His expression was calm yet stern, exuding an air of authority and grace.

"I am Sir Lancelot du Lac," the knight introduced himself, his voice resonating with a regal tone. "Akira, you are my long-lost heir. Along with Isabella and two others, you must unite to face Luca, the descendant of Morgana. The fate of the world rests upon your shoulders."

Akira was stunned, struggling to process the reality of what he was experiencing. Yet, the presence of the legendary knight before him made it hard to deny. Lancelot continued, "In this journey, you will need a weapon worthy of your lineage. You must go to the golden temple nestled among the tranquil gardens, where shimmering koi swim beneath the arched bridges. It is there where you will find the spear that once belonged to me. It is there, waiting for you to claim it."

As Lancelot spoke, a vision formed before Akira's eyes, revealing the magnificent Golden Pavilion, gleaming in the sunlight amidst a tranquil pond, its reflection shimmering in the water. The vision faded, and Akira found himself back in the dojo, the ancient scroll still clutched in his hands.

Akira stood in the center of the dojo, still reeling from his encounter with Sir Lancelot and the surreal vision. He turned to face Isabella and Master Takashi, his expression a mixture of astonishment and determination. Taking a deep breath, he began to recount the incredible experience he had just undergone. As he described the sudden transportation to the ancient temple, the appearance of Sir Lancelot, and the message about uniting with the other heirs, Isabella listened with captivated attention. Her eyes widened, and a look of shock crossed her face, but it was quickly replaced by an expression of excitement. She felt a thrill of confirmation, the pieces of their mysterious mission beginning to fall into place. Her heart raced with the realization that their journey was truly unfolding in ways she had not fully imagined before.

Master Takashi, on the other hand, listened in silence, his face calm yet thoughtful. Although the story seemed fantastical and beyond comprehension, he could see the earnestness in Akira's eyes. There had always been something special about Akira, a certain aura that set him apart from his other students.

He placed a reassuring hand on Akira's shoulder. "It seems that fate has chosen you for a significant journey. I may not fully understand it, but I believe in you. Embrace this destiny and face it with the honor and courage I know you possess."

Isabella glanced at Akira, feeling a renewed sense of purpose and camaraderie. They were connected now, bound by a mission that transcended ordinary life. The excitement in her eyes reflected the anticipation of the challenges and discoveries that lay ahead. She felt a surge of energy, ready to continue their quest and find the remaining heirs.

Isabella looked at Akira with a confident yet gentle expression. Her presence radiated an aura of leadership and determination, qualities that were becoming more apparent with each passing moment. She met his gaze and, with a slight smile, asked, "So, do you believe me now?"

Akira, still processing everything but feeling a strange mix of excitement and nervousness, let out a soft chuckle. A playful grin spread across his face as he nodded. "I guess that means we're off to the island of the rising sun, huh? This is going to be one hell of an adventure", he replied. There was a sincerity in his tone, tempered with a lightheartedness that eased the weight of their newfound mission. Their journey was beginning to feel real, and despite the unknowns ahead, there was an undeniable spark of excitement in the air.

After a long journey across the ocean, Isabella and Akira arrived just outside the golden temple under the cover of darkness; their journey filled with anticipation and an understanding of the gravity of their mission. Knowing the significance of the sacred artifact hidden within the temple, they decided to approach it at night to avoid drawing attention. The golden temple's serene reflection by the moonlit in a pond made it appear otherworldly, almost of mystical solemn amidst the quiet of the night.

As the moon reached its zenith, casting a silver glow over the landscape, Isabella and Akira stood before the temple's grand entrance. The air was crisp, filled with the faint scent of pine and Cherrie Blossom trees and the sound of rustling leaves. With a deep breath, Isabella pushed open the heavy doors. The hinges creaked softly, revealing the temple's interior. They stepped inside, only to find an unexpected sight of emptiness. The hall was silent,

William Henry Belmont

devoid of any mystical aura or ancient artifacts. It was just an ordinary temple, with woven mats and modest decorations. There was no sign of the sacred spear or anything extraordinary.

Disheartened and confused, they stepped back outside to gather their thoughts. The cool night air filled their lungs as they stood beneath the starry sky. Akira's mind wandered back to his early training days with Master Takashi. He recalled a lesson that had always stayed with him: "A man's true enemy is doubt. When the time comes, you must prove who you are on your own." The words resonated deeply within him, now more than ever.

Turning to Isabella, Akira spoke with fresh resolve. "I think this is something I need to do alone," he said, his voice steady but gentle. "Master Takashi always said that doubt is the real enemy, and maybe… maybe the temple won't reveal its secrets until I prove myself. I need to show that I am not afraid."

Isabella studied his face for a moment, seeing the determination in his eyes. She nodded in agreement, understanding the significance of his decision. "I'll be right here, waiting," she reassured him, her voice full of support. As he was turning around to face the door, he hears Isabella's voice saying "please, be careful." Akira locked his eyes with hers and smile. This time, it was Akira who pushed open the door, stepping inside alone. As the door closed behind him, Isabella watched, feeling a mix of anticipation and hope. She knew this was a crucial moment for Akira, a test not just of bravery but of belief in himself and the path they were on. As the door closed, Isabella's beautiful silhouette disappeared, leaving Akira alone inside the temple.

As Akira stepped into the temple, the air shifted. The vast hall dissolved into an endless void stretching beyond sight. In front of him stood two figures, Isabella and Master Takashi, each bound by thick, shadowy chains, their heads bowed. Between them, on an ornate pedestal, rested the sacred spear, its surface gleaming with an otherworldly light.

From the darkness, an armored samurai emerged. His presence was suffocating, radiating an ancient, oppressive force. His helmet concealed his face, but his voice cut through the silence like a blade. "The path of the warrior is paved with sacrifice."

A ring of spectral blades rose around Isabella and Takashi, hovering just above their throats.

Akira's breath caught. In a panic, he rushed to Master Takashi, clawing at the chains around his neck, but they held firmly. He turned to Isabella, trying desperately to break her bonds, but again, he failed.

The samurai laughed, the sound cold and hollow. "Take the spear and choose, your friend or your master. You cannot save both."

Akira's hands trembled.

"Take the spear and save your master," Isabella pleaded, tears rolling down her face. "You barely know me."

Akira looked at her, horrified.

Master Takashi's gaze was steady. "Do not doubt yourself, Akira. You are meant for something greater." His voice was calm, unwavering. "Take the spear and save the girl. I have lived long enough."

The spectral blades inched closer, drawing thin lines of blood against their skin.

Akira's heart pounded. He grabbed the spear and struck the chains, again and again, but they would not break.

The samurai's laughter echoed once more. "Foolish boy. You don't get everything you want. Choose, or I will choose for you."

The blades pressed closer. The trickle of blood grew.

The samurai's voice deepened, reverberating through the void. "The spear demands a blood sacrifice to serve its new master."

Akira's grip tightened around the spear. His expression hardened. "So be it."

He turned to Isabella, his eyes fierce with conviction.

"Take the spear and finish the mission."

Before she could react, Akira raised the spear and slit his own throat.

Akira slowly awakens and finds himself lying on the cold floor of the temple. His heart was still racing, his body aching from the ordeal. He looked up and saw the spear, pristine and powerful, resting on a table in the middle of the room.

Akira gasped, his hands flying to his throat. But there were no wounds. No blood. Only the lingering sensation of cold steel against his skin. He staggered to his feet, disoriented. His breath was ragged, his mind reeling from what had just happened. Had he died? Had it all been real?

Then, out of the corner of his eye, he noticed a figure seated in the far-right corner of the temple, Sir Lancelot. The knight watched him with a knowing gaze, his expression unreadable.

Akira's voice was hoarse. "Was it real? Isabella and Master Takashi, are they still trapped?"

Lancelot exhaled slowly, leaning forward. "They are safe."

Akira's fists clenched. "Was it, all just some illusion?"

Lancelot met his gaze, unshaken. "Your trial was never about what was real, it was about what you would do."

The weight of the words settled over Akira like a stone. His legs felt weak. The memories of the trial still burned in his mind, the fear, the choice, the sacrifice. Even if it had not been real, the choice had been.

Lancelot stood, walking toward him. "Now you understand. The spear is not claimed by strength alone, but by the heart that wields it. And you, Akira, chose selflessness over power. Please, take the spear, it is yours." Sir Lancelot said.

Akira walked over to the table and reached out with both arms to take the spear. As his hands grasped the weapon, he felt a surge of power course through him.

Suddenly, a powerful gust of wind swirled around the spear in Akira's hand, lifting the ends of his hair. The spear glowed with a radiant light, illuminating the area with a mystical aura. As the wind intensified, the spear began to transform, its solid form shifting and changing. The spear's metallic surface shimmered, morphing into a sleek and elegant bracelet.

The bracelet was crafted from shiny silver, its surface polished to perfection, catching the light with every movement. It was adorned with brilliant blue sapphires, each gemstone set meticulously into the band. The sapphires gleamed like drops of the purest water, their deep blue color reminiscent of the ocean's depths. The bracelet's design was both intricate and sturdy, with subtle engravings that flowed along the silver like the wind itself. It was a piece of jewelry that exuded both beauty and strength.

Sir Lancelot stepped forward. "Place this bracelet on your arm," he instructed, his voice carrying the weight of ancient wisdom. "Let its power course through you. When you most need it, the spear will appear in its place."

Akira took the bracelet. As he held it, he felt a subtle hum of energy emanating from the silver band. He carefully placed the bracelet on his right wrist, feeling its cool touch against his skin. The bracelet fit perfectly, as if it had been made just for him. As soon as it settled into place, the sapphires glowed faintly, and a rush of energy surged through him. He felt a powerful connection to the wind, as if he could command it with a mere thought. The sensation was exhilarating, filling him with a sense of boundless potential and power.

As he approached the exit, Sir Lancelot's voice called out to him one last time, "Tell the young lady waiting outside that door," Sir Lancelot instructed, "you two must go to the old world and find the greatest sword that ever existed, only with it, and its wielder can you hope to save the world." With a warm smile, Sir Lancelot faded away, his presence dissipating like a dream.

Akira opened the door of the temple, and there stood Isabella, her eyes filled with a mixture of hope, happiness, and perhaps something deeper. She met his gaze with a soft smile, her rosy cheeks revealing a warmth that mirrored her admiration for him. As he stepped through the doorway, bracelet on his arm, their silence acknowledging the unspoken bond growing between them. Akira smiled back at Isabella, touched by her presence, almost feeling a purifying sense thanks to her. With a gentle touch, he closed the door behind him, leaving the past behind, hoping for a better future.

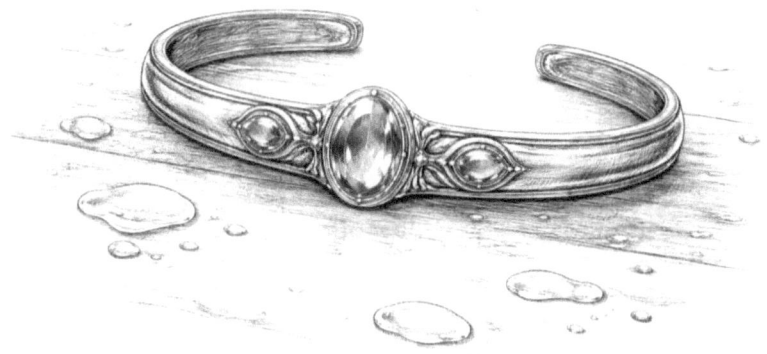

William Henry Belmont

Part 3: The Corrupt Heir

.

Meanwhile, in a different part of our world, a man paces along his study, a space that exudes modern luxury. The room was a blend of sleek, minimalist design and lavish finishes. The walls were adorned with abstract art pieces, and the shelves were full of rare books and antique artifacts. A large, plush leather sofa sat in the center of the room, facing a low glass coffee table. The floor was made of polished dark wood, reflecting the ambient lighting from contemporary chandeliers above.

A servant entered quietly, carrying a silver tray and placed it gently on the coffee table. "Your beverage, sir," the servant said, his voice more apprehensive than respectful. The man barely acknowledged him, a look of mild annoyance crossing his face. Without looking at the servant, he slurred, "About time," as if the servant's presence was an inconvenience. He took the drink and sipped it, continuing to pace and think.

William Henry Belmont

The man was striking, with short blonde hair and piercing blue eyes that bordered on grey. His features were chiseled, giving him a naturally handsome appearance. He wore an impeccably tailored suit that emphasized his athletic build, evidence of his wealth and status. As he walked, his demeanor radiated arrogance and a sense of superiority.

As the man paced his study, with the restless certainty of someone who believes the world belonged to him, he suddenly stopped. He stood by the window, watching the servants' children play across the far edge of his vast estate, near the low dwellings built for those meant to serve. As their laughter carried faintly through the glass, he closed his eyes, and his mind drifted, unwillingly, back to another time.

In a beautiful green garden, surrounded by tall trees and manicured shrubs, a pale-skinned boy no older than twelve stood awkwardly, dressed in expensive clothing. His blonde hair was neatly combed, though now ruffled from confrontation. He stood tall, but timid, as he tried to defend himself from three boys his age. They wore threaded shirts and muddy boots; their hands and faces streaked with dirt.

"We're not going to play with you," said the leader of the trio, his voice filled with sneering certainty. "Our parents told us about you… and your family."

The other two boys snickered behind him.

"What's wrong with me or my family?" the blonde boy asked, confusion flickering across his face.

The leader stepped forward. "You're not one of us. You play with your servants, with your expensive toys and trinkets. You talk like you own everything."

Then he shoved him.

The blonde boy fell into the mud, scraping his palms on gravel hidden beneath the grass. A few tears escaped before he could stop them, tracing down his pale cheeks. His lip trembled. The other boys laughed, mocking him, not with cruelty, but

William Henry Belmont

with the casual disdain of children already taught whom to hate.

It was the first time they pushed him into the mud.

They were sons of merchants and laborers, children of the city's middle and lower quarters. They had been raised, perhaps without knowing it, to resent what they did not have. They hated his polished boots, the way his jacket caught the light, the fine ring on his finger. But most of all, they hated how he looked at the world, like it owed him something.

He didn't intend to cry at first when they shoved him. Not at first. But when one of them spit on his coat, and the others laughed again, something inside him broke.

His fists clenched. His eyes burned. But he said nothing.

He walked home in silence, skin scraped, coat ruined, heart quietly changed.

Later that evening, he sat at the long dining table of his family estate. His sleeves were still stained with dirt. He hadn't spoken a word since returning.

His mother entered, tall and elegant, dressed in silk the color of moonlight. Her heels tapped softly on the marble floor.

She stopped when she saw him.

"You let those boys touch you amore mio?" she asked, her voice cold as polished steel.

He didn't answer.

"You cried, didn't you?"

He looked down.

She stepped closer, lifted his chin with two fingers, gently, but with force.

"Never cry," she said, her voice as sharp as glass. "Feelings are for the weak. Do you hear me?"

He nodded slowly.

"You are not like them. You are of a bloodline older than this city. You were born to command. And those who command," she added, brushing a fleck of dirt from his cuff, "do not ask. They take."

She looked at the mud still caked on his coat, then smiled faintly.

"Those boys... do you know what they are?"

William Henry Belmont

He hesitated.

She didn't.

"They are less than animals."

Her eyes glinted with pride as she leaned in close.

"And what do we do to animals who bite?"

He hesitated again. Then, quietly: "…We put them down."

She kissed him lightly on the forehead and stood.

"That's my son."

His mind back in the present, leaving the study, he wandered through the corridors of his grand mansion, a symbol of his generational wealth. The walls were adorned with portraits of his ancestors, and the halls were lined with priceless sculptures and tapestries. He made his way to a heavily secure door, behind which lay his family's vault. The vault was a treasure trove of heirlooms, collector's items, and precious artifacts, accumulated over generations. The man walked slowly, admiring the gleaming treasures around him, each piece proof to his family's legacy. He paused to touch a golden artifact, a satisfied smile playing on his lips, reveling in the power and privilege that had been his birthright.

As he walked through his home, admiring the wealth he possessed. He inspected his labor force, cleaning, tending the gardens, and preparing his meals. He took a slow breath, measured and deliberate, his thoughts turning inward. His eyes closed as memory stirred, carrying him back to his father and mother, and to the lessons they had carved into him long ago.

A young man in his late teens stands tall, his posture composed, his hands folded neatly behind his back. He was striking, handsome, poised, and already carrying the quiet arrogance of someone who had been taught his worth since birth.

Beside him walked his father, older but immensely more commanding. Together they strolled through the grand halls of their estate, inspecting the servants as they worked. The air carried the scents of polished wood and fresh herbs from the kitchens. Outside the tall windows, gardeners trimmed the hedges with careful precision. Inside, maids swept, dusted, and moved like shadows across the marble floors.

As the two men passed, all the servants lowered their eyes, avoiding direct contact. They had been taught well. Eye contact was not a right afforded to those below.

Then, a small disturbance occurred.

One servant, a thin man carrying a tray with food, caught his foot on the edge of an ornate rug. The tray slipped from his hands and clattered to the floor, the sound echoing off the stone walls. Bowls shattered. Silence followed.

The father stopped. His eyes, sharp and unforgiving, fixed on the trembling servant.

"Gather your belongings," he said coldly. "And leave my house."

The servant, pale with fear, fell to his knees. "Please, my lord," he said, his voice cracking. "My family, my children, we need this work."

The man's voice did not rise. It did not need to.

"I said leave."

There was no anger in his tone. Only certainty.

The servant bowed his head, his tears falling silently onto the floor, and left without another word.

The young man watched, his brow creased with something between curiosity and doubt. He turned to his father as they resumed walking.

"Was it necessary?" he asked quietly. "Could you not have given him another chance?"

The father glanced at him, amused. "Necessary?" he repeated, as though tasting the word.

"It is necessary that you understand this: those who serve us learn better through fear than through love."

The young man absorbed the words in silence.

"But what about respect?" he asked after a pause.

William Henry Belmont

His father's eyes narrowed, not in rage but in disdain, annoyed that the question even needed to be asked.

"Respect," he said, "is an illusion."

They stopped at the edge of the great hall, the sun casting golden light through high windows onto the polished floor.

"When you give orders," the father continued, his voice low and deliberate, "you give them once. If they disobey, you punish swiftly. Never explain yourself. Never ask twice. The moment they believe you need their loyalty more than they need your favor…" He leaned in slightly. "…you are no longer their master."

The young man said nothing. He stood still, thoughtful, watching the hallway where the servant had vanished. A part of him, the part that once asked questions, grew quieter.

His father placed a hand on his shoulder.

"One day," he said, "all of this will be yours."

The young man nodded slowly.

And he kept watching.

Learning everything.

As the man continued to walk his vault and admire his collection, a peculiar sensation of urgency tugged at him from one corner of the vault. His gaze followed the invisible pull to a small, worn desk made of blackish wood. A desk that he could have sworn he has never seen before. The desk stood in contrast to the polished luxury around it, appearing almost out of place among the gleaming treasures. On its surface lay a few loose pieces of yellowed paper and an old inkwell with a quill still resting in it, as if frozen in time.

Curiosity set in, he approached the desk and opened the center drawer. Inside, he found a small ebony jewelry chest, its surface covered in a thick layer of dust and cobwebs, suggesting it had been untouched for years. The chest seemed mysterious to say the least, and as he lifted it from the drawer, he felt a strange sense of power and belonging emanating from it. He blew away

William Henry Belmont

the dust and cobwebs, revealing its dark, polished surface.

Slowly, almost reverently, he opened the chest. Inside, resting on an emerald-colored cushion, was a beautiful black ring adorned with a dark, enigmatic red stone. The ring's design was intricate and elegant, with an aura of mystery that drew him in. He picked it up with his left hand, feeling the cool weight of the metal. The jewelry chest was returned to the drawer without a second glance, his focus entirely on the ring.

As he brought the ring closer to his eyes, he marveled at its exquisite craftsmanship and the deep, captivating hue of the stone. Suddenly, an overwhelming urge to wear the ring surged within him. Without hesitation, he slipped the ring onto the index finger of his right hand. The moment the ring settled on his finger, he felt a rush of energy course through him, intensifying the sense of power and destiny he had always felt but never fully understood.

As the man felt the powerful energy emanating from the ring, a shadowy and mysterious woman emerged before him. She was strikingly beautiful, dressed in a long, completely black tunic and robe that seemed to absorb the light around her. Her skin was as white as ivory, contrasting sharply with her long, sleek black hair that cascaded down her back. Her piercing blue eyes, filled with malice, sparkled with an unsettling allure, exuding both beauty and danger.

Though the man appeared slightly confused by her sudden appearance, there was a hint of anticipation or excitement in his demeanor, as if he had been expecting her arrival. Their eyes locked, and then her gaze shifted down to his hand, where the ring gleamed ominously. "If you are wearing my ring, then you are the descendant I have been waiting for," she said, her voice cold yet captivating, with an almost sensual undertone.

Still gazing into her eyes, he replied, "Am I the one you seek?" His voice carried

William Henry Belmont

a mix of curiosity and challenge. "And who might you be?" he asked, the question laced with a subtle provocation.

The woman began to move around the vault, her steps graceful yet deliberate, as if she were assessing her surroundings. After a moment, she stopped and turned to him, a look of disdain crossing her face. "You insolent fool," she hissed, her voice growing colder. "I am the most powerful witch that has ever existed." Her eyes burned with intensity as she continued, "My name is Morgana Le Fay," she roared, her presence filling the room with an overwhelming sense of dark power.

The man took a step back, a drop of fear crossing his face, yet his chest swelled with excitement and anticipation. "My apologies, my lady," he said, his tone respectful for the first time in his life. "I have read about you in the books passed down by my family. I thought you were nothing more than a story told to children so they could sleep," he continued, struggling to reconcile the legend with the reality before him.

Morgana's eyes narrowed, her expression a mixture of disdain and amusement. "Neither my magic nor your fate are mere stories," she replied, her voice dripping with an ominous certainty. With a wave of her hand, the wealthy surroundings of the mansion vanished, replaced by the haunting scene of a ruined city still smoldering with flames. The air was thick with the unpleasant scent of smoke and destruction.

As the man looked around in shock, his gaze settled on a younger Morgana standing proudly amidst the chaos. She was even more beautiful than before, displaying an aura of power and dominance. In her hand, she held a long, black, and intricately designed magical staff with a red dark stone at its tip, pulsating with a mysterious energy.

Before her stood four men. Three were clad in splendid, shining armor, each holding a weapon: one a sword, another a spear, and the third an axe. The fourth figure, an older man, wore a dark blue robe and clutched an ancient book. The younger Morgana's eyes gleamed with dark intent as she faced them, her presence commanding and formidable. The scene was a representation of a pivotal moment in history, now revealed as a chilling reality.

Suddenly, the man and Morgana were back in the vault. Morgana paced back and forth, her expression a storm of anger and frustration. "If it weren't for those four fools, I would have conquered the world," she hissed, her voice seething with bitterness. "Now it is up to you to conquer the world in my name."

The man's lips curled into a smile, as if he had just been given the opportunity he had longed for his entire life. Morgana continued, almost as if she had forgotten his presence, "Undoubtedly, that old fool must have known I would have a plan to continue my conquest." She paused, turning her gaze towards him. "If you are to succeed, you will need my staff. You need it to destroy whatever Merlin has conjured to stop you from claiming the world as your own." The man listened intently, savoring every word. He felt a growing excitement, as if he was finally stepping into the destiny he had always believed was his. "Very well, where can I get that staff?" he asked, his voice filled with anticipation.

Morgana looked at him closely, a sly smile spreading across her face. "You already have it. It's in your hand, right there," she said, pointing to the ring on his finger.

The man looked down at the ring, then back at Morgana, a frown of confusion crossing his face as he struggled to understand her words. Morgana approached him slowly, her movements graceful and deliberate. She lifted his chin with one hand, forcing their eyes to meet. Her touch was both gentle and commanding, a subtle seduction. "The staff will manifest to you whenever you need it," she whispered, her voice laced with a dangerous allure. "But it's not enough to simply wear the ring. You must do something for me."

William Henry Belmont

As she spoke, he felt an overwhelming pull toward her, his lips almost brushing hers, lost in her captivating presence. Just as he was about to close the distance, Morgana pulled away, taking a step back. The tension between them was palpable. "I will do whatever you wish me to do," he said, a smile spreading across his face, filled with a dark eagerness.

With a wave of her hand, the scene around them changed in an instant. They were now standing in a lavish and wealthy bedroom, still within the mansion's luxurious confines. The room was adorned with rich tapestries and expensive furniture. At the center of the room stood a grand bed, draped with elegant, flowing curtains.

Morgana turned to face him, her expression serene but her eyes glinting with malevolent intent. "Kill her for me," she commanded, her voice sweet yet chilling. The words hung in the air; a sinister request veiled in a tone of sexuality.

The man met Morgana's gaze with a look of unwavering certainty. He walked around the bed and sat on its edge, beside his sleeping wife. Without a second thought, he reached over to the nightstand, opened the drawer, and retrieved a small, ornate dagger that gleamed with a deadly elegance. Slowly, he raised the dagger above his head, his movements deliberate and precise. Without hesitation, he plunged the blade directly into the woman's heart. She let out a small gasp, her eyes fluttering open for a brief, agonizing moment as blood blossomed across her white nightgown. Her life ended instantly.

It is clear that the man had never felt anything for her, he has never felt anything for anyone, until this day. He stood up, the dagger still in his hand, its blade now stained with crimson. Blood dripped onto the luxurious carpet below. When he looked up, his eyes met Morgana's. She was smiling, an evil smile that sent a chill through the room. Her expression was one of triumph and

William Henry Belmont

satisfaction, a dark acknowledgment of the monstrous act he had just committed.

Morgana walked towards the man with a seductive grace; her eyes locked onto his. "Luca Faerie, the full power of the ring is now yours," she purred, her voice a hot whisper that sent shivers down his spine. She continued to move closer, her presence intoxicating and alluring. "Take my staff and all my power, and fulfill our destiny," she commanded, now standing directly in front of him.

With a fluid motion, she wrapped her arms around his neck, pulling him into an intimate embrace. He reciprocated, his hands resting on her hips as their bodies pressed together. They drew closer still, their lips meeting in a passionate kiss that ignited a dark, electric energy around them. Red lightning bolts crackled through the air, illuminating the room in an ominous glow as they continued to kiss, their connection deepening with every second.

Morgana felt a surge of triumph and power, knowing her plan was unfolding perfectly. The man, in turn, felt an intoxicating mix of power and dark desire, a feeling unlike anything he had ever experienced. The room filled with a potent blend of evil, power, and raw temptation, their union sealing a pact that promised a future steeped in darkness and conquest. As the red lightning crackled and the air pulsed with dark energy, it was clear that a new menace to the world had just awakened.

As Morgana's apparition faded before him, Luca's lips curled into a sinister smile, his thoughts drifting back to another moment from his past.

The storm had not yet broken, yet dark clouds covered the sky, thunder forming in the distance, low and patient, like a beast deciding when to strike.

The blonde man entered the study with urgency in his steps. The heavy oak doors closed behind him with a dull thud.

His father was already seated behind his great desk. His mother stood beside him, draped in silk like a statue brought to life, her hand resting with poised elegance on the back of her husband's chair.

The young man spoke first.

"There's a mob outside," he said, voice tight with purpose. "Peasants. They're shouting your name. They say… they say they've had enough. That the food shortage is more than they can bear."

The father didn't answer. Not at first.

He rose slowly from his chair, as though his movements were chosen for their weight, not their haste. He walked to the tall window, where the candlelight barely reached. Beyond the glass, shadows stirred torches, shapes, muffled voices in the fog.

He watched them for a long time.

"They're angry," his son said again. "They want answers."

Still, the father said nothing. His hands folded behind his back.

"Being responsible for the lives of this city," he said finally, "is a heavy burden."

He paced slowly, tracing the edge of the rug with deliberate steps. The fire crackled softly behind them.

"Some people believe they know what they want," he said, gesturing vaguely toward the window. "They cry for freedom, for justice. But listen closely, what they really want is to be rescued."

He returned to his chair and sat once more, his posture regal, calm.

His wife spoke next, her voice smooth and unwavering.

"Dogs," she murmured, "pretending to be wolves."

The young man turned to her. A faint smirk formed at the corner of his mouth.

"Let me tell you a story," the mother said.

Her voice dropped low, entrancing, like the beginning of a prayer meant only for those willing to believe.

"There was once a village where every man's voice was equal," she began. "They had no ruler. No law. Every decision was made together."

William Henry Belmont

She moved slowly across the room, her gown brushing the stone like silk over steel.

"At first, it worked. They shared water. Break bread. Voted on planting, harvesting. Everything was discussed. Everything was fair."

She turned, eyes falling on her son.

"But then one man asked for more water than his share. Another demanded a larger house. One desired his neighbor's wife. And another… refused to work at all. Said he deserved rest while others labored."

She paused.

"They argued. Shouted. The votes turned into fights. Fists into blades. In the end, they burned their homes. Poisoned their wells. Salted the soil beneath their feet."

From the chair, her husband added quietly, "Only a few survived."

The mother's gaze lingered on her son.

"Starving. Desperate. They prayed to the skies, not for rain. Not for mercy. But for an answer."

Outside, thunder rolled again, closer now. A hush fell over the study.

"And then," she said, "a stranger came down from a distant land. He gave them laws. Gave them roles. Named one a baker. Another, a builder. Another, a soldier. And he punished those who broke the order."

She stepped beside the fire.

"Within a few years, the village was quiet. The soil grew rich again. And the people lived… not free, but fed. Not equal, but content."

Her husband nodded, not at her, but at the story, as though it had always belonged to him.

"These people," he said, "do not want to lead. They want someone else to make the decisions, so they can pretend they still have a voice."

He leaned back in his chair, hands steepled.

"Choice is terrifying, son. Far more than hunger."

Outside, the storm cracked like a warning shot across the sky.

William Henry Belmont

He looked his son in the eyes.

"Understand this," he said softly. "When the world begins to burn… they will not run to the freeman."

A pause.

"They will run to the strongman."

The mother moved closer now, resting a hand gently on her son's shoulder.

"They will beg," she whispered, smiling faintly. "And they will call it loyalty."

The young man stood still, his gaze fixed on the darkened window.

His reflection stared back, calm, composed, listening.

He said nothing.

And as the storm broke above the mansion, and the rain began to pour in veils across the earth, something inside him shifted.

No doubt.

Not fear.

Certainty.

The certainty that some were born to be led.

And he, was meant to lead them.

Morgana has found her perfect student, someone to carve her name into permanence. Luca smiles as he has found an infinite source of power and knowledge.

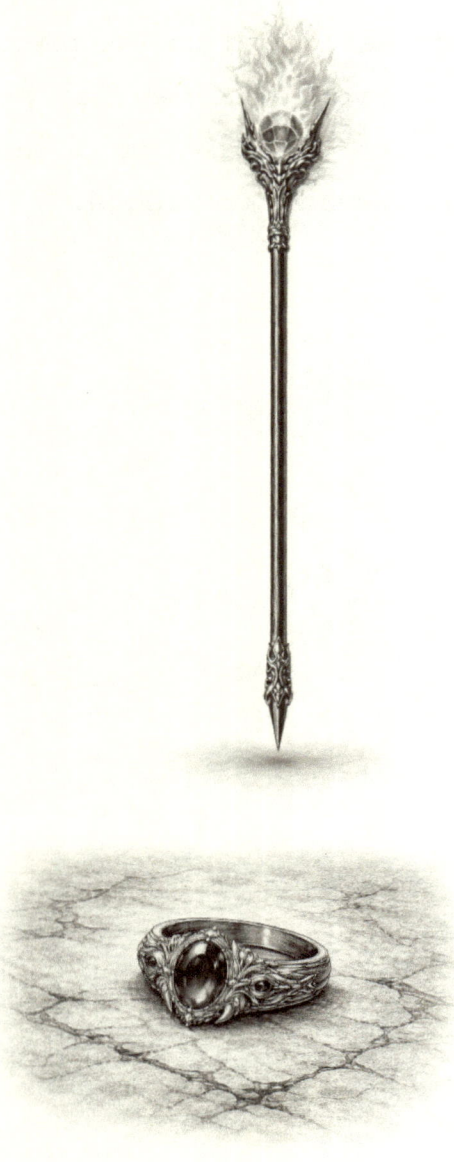

Echoes of Legends

Part 4: The Blande's Descendant

William Henry Belmont

As Isabella and Akira arrived at the land of old kingdoms, they found themselves pondering the cryptic clue Sir Lancelot had given them: they must find the greatest sword that ever existed and its wielder. This enigmatic message set Isabella's mind racing, sifting through the vast array of historical and mythical swords she had encountered in her studies. One legendary blade quickly came to her mind, the sword in the stone.

Isabella explained the tale to Akira as they walked through the old-fashioned streets of a small old town. "The legend goes that whoever could pull the sword from the stone was destined to be the next king of all the land," she began. "The only person who ever accomplished this feat was King Arthur. It is said that Merlin, the legendary wizard, originally obtained the sword from the Lady of the Lake, a mystical water goddess who aided him. This powerful sword was known as Excalibur."

She paused, looking thoughtful. "Excalibur was not just a symbol of royalty, but a blade imbued with incredible power. However, as far as most people know, this story is just a myth, a beautiful tale passed down through generations. But now, with everything we've encountered, I'm beginning to wonder if there's more truth to these legends than we've been led to believe."

Akira listened intently, his expression, a mix of curiosity and intrigue. "So, where do we find Excalibur? If it's even real, that is."

Isabella nodded, acknowledging the uncertainty. "That's the tricky part. Most people believe Excalibur is just a legend, and even if it did exist, it would have been lost to time. However, there's a famous replica on display at Tintagel Castle, a site steeped in Arthurian lore. It's a popular tourist attraction where visitors can admire the sword and learn about its supposed history. But, as far as anyone knows, it's just that, a replica, a piece of fiction made tangible for the sake of storytelling."

She paused, then added, "Given everything we've seen and experienced, we can't dismiss the possibility that the real Excalibur, or at least something connected to it, might be there. We should go to Tintagel Castle and see if we can find any clues about the sword or its rightful wielder."

With their course set, Isabella and Akira made their way to Tintagel Castle, hopeful that they might uncover the truth behind the legend and perhaps meet the next heir destined to wield the legendary Excalibur.

As they arrived at the Castle, Isabella and Akira were taken aback by its beauty and magnificence. The castle, perched atop rugged cliffs overlooking the sea, seemed to rise majestically from the green hills that surrounded it. The waves crashed against the rocks below, creating a symphony of natural sounds that added to the mystical ambiance of the place. The castle's ancient stone walls, partially weathered by time, told tales of a bygone eras filled with legends and lore. The rolling hills, lush and vibrant, stretched out as far as the eye could see, creating a picturesque backdrop for this legendary site.

As they walked inside the castle, they noticed a group of travelers gathered around a guide near a sword embedded in a stone. From a distance, they could hear the local guide passionately recounting the lore behind the sword. "And here, we have the famous sword… Excalibur," the guide announced, his voice carrying through the crowd. "The legend says that only the true king of the land can pull this sword from the stone. According to the myth, young Arthur was the only one who could perform this feat, proving his right to the throne."

This young guide stands at about six feet tall, his blond hair, falling normally just above his shoulders, tied back with a simple hair tie. His light blue eyes hold quiet skepticism, and his features are handsome but not striking. Fit but not overly muscular, he carries himself with relaxed confidence, unaware of anything remarkable about himself.

He playfully taunted several people in the crowd, inviting them to try their luck at pulling the sword from the stone. Laughter echoed through the air as one by one, the travelers tugged at the hilt, each failing to budge the blade even an inch. The guide grinned and, with a dramatic flourish, made his own attempt, only to be met with the same result. "Well, it seems I shall remain but a humble guide," he joked, eliciting chuckles from the crowd. He then gestured for the group to follow him to another part of the castle, leaving the sword momentarily unattended.

Seizing the opportunity, Isabella and Akira approached the sword. It was an old, rusted relic, firmly lodged in the stone. The stone itself bore a plaque with an inscription that read, "Whosoever shall draw this sword from this stone is the rightful King of all this land." They stood there, admiring the sword and pondering the legend.

Echoes of Legends

Could this truly be the legendary Excalibur, or merely a well-crafted replica?

As they were lost in thought, the guide returned. He noticed them standing by the sword and offered a warm smile. "Interesting legend, innit?" he asked, his eyes twinkling with a hint of curiosity. "Do you have any questions about the sword or its history?" His tone was inviting, and there was an air of genuine enthusiasm in his voice, as if he relished the opportunity to share the stories of the past.

Isabella hesitated for a moment, then spoke up, "Well, si, as odd as this may sound to you, is there any truth to the legend? Is this the real Excalibur?" The guide smiled warmly, "That would be nice, wouldn't it?" he responded, a hint of amusement in his voice. "But it's just a story. My parents told it to me, and their parents told it to them." Isabella glanced at Akira, slightly disappointed.

Akira turned to the guide and said, "Well, thank you." The guide nodded amiably and introduced himself, "My name is

William Henry Belmont

Pendrick, by the way, William Pendrick. Please let me know if there's anything more you need." With that, the guide walked away, leaving them by the sword.

As he walked away, Akira looked at Isabella and said, "we tried, but it was a long shot." Just then, Isabella noticed something unusual: Akira's bracelet was glowing. At the same moment, Akira noticed her pendant glowing as well. They both felt a sudden and incredible sense of belonging, realizing they were in the right place. They exchanged a knowing look, feeling a strange connection to the guide, William.

Determined, they decided to find William again and return to the sword. As they spoke to him, they continued to question the authenticity of the sword, pressing him for any hint that it might be real. William, initially patient, grew increasingly annoyed with their persistence. "Look," he finally said, a hint of frustration in his voice, "it's just a story."

As William spoke, he placed his hand on the hilt of the sword, dismissing their questions with a hint of impatience. "Believe me, it's just a story. The sword is fake, and it's fixed to the stone." But as he wrapped his fingers around the hilt, Isabella and Akira's jewelry began to glow even more intensely, as if resonating with the energy of the sword. The air felt charged, like an acknowledgment of a long-awaited reunion.

Determined to prove his point, William pulled on the hilt with a firm tug. To his astonishment, the sword slid out of the stone effortlessly. The unexpected momentum sent him stumbling backward, and he fell to the ground, still clutching the sword. The hilt of the still rusty blade glowed slightly, the same ethereal glow emanating from the bracelet and pendant.

Isabella and Akira stood frozen in shock, unable to comprehend what they had just witnessed. The sword was supposed to be a mere prop, a fixed piece of the castle's lore. Yet, here it was, free from the stone, held in the hands of a seemingly ordinary tour guide. William slowly stood up, his eyes wide with disbelief. "What is going on?" he muttered to himself, utterly bewildered. His voice was tinged with a mix of confusion and intrigue.

As William stood there, visibly perplexed, Isabella took a step closer, her voice calm and sincere. She explained their journey, the magical nature of their mission, and the significance of the sword he now held. She spoke of the legendary weapons they carried, once wielded by the knights of old, and how they had transformed into the jewelry they now wore. Akira nodded in agreement, adding details about the trials they had faced and the powerful forces they were meant to counter.

William listened intently, his gaze shifting between Isabella and Akira. The story was fantastical, filled with elements he had only ever read about in myths and legends. He glanced down at the sword in his hand, its appearance far from awe-inspiring. The blade was tarnished and worn, more reminiscent of a discarded relic than an all-powerful weapon of legend. The hilt, however, continued to emit a soft, magical glow, as did Isabella's pendant and Akira's bracelet.

Despite the eerie coincidence of the glowing jewelry and the sword's release from the stone, William couldn't fully embrace the story. He was a man of practical thoughts, grounded in reality, and the idea of being part of a magical quest seemed absurd. "It doesn't look like anything special," he muttered, inspecting the rusted metal. "It's just an old, rusty piece of metal." His skepticism was evident, though there was a glimmer of curiosity in his eyes. The strange circumstances surrounding the sword and the jewelry's glow intrigued him, even if he couldn't yet believe in the story's full extent.

William's voice dripped with disdain as he held up the sword for Isabella and Akira to see. "This cannot be the real Excalibur," he scoffed, glancing at the dull, rusted blade. "Look at it" With a

William Henry Belmont

dismissive gesture, he practically threw the sword back into the stone. The moment the blade settled into its resting place, the bracelet on Akira's wrist and the pendant around Isabella's neck began to shine with an even more intense light.

The radiance quickly grew blinding, forcing all three to shield their eyes. As the light gradually dimmed, they cautiously uncovered their eyes, blinking to adjust to the sudden darkness. Slowly, their vision returned, revealing the ghostly figures of Sir Percival and Sir Lancelot standing before them, their forms shimmering with a spectral glow.

Sir Lancelot stepped forward, his face a mask of anger and authority. He pointed at William, his voice commanded, "You insolent little thing! That is no way to treat King Arthur's sword!" His words echoed with a righteous fury, as the castle seemed to tremble under their weight. The ghostly knight's eyes burned with a fierce intensity, conveying the importance and sacredness of the weapon William had so carelessly dismissed. The atmosphere was thick with a mix of awe and tension, as the gravity of the situation settled over them all.

Isabella and Akira, though initially taken aback by the sudden appearance of the ghostly knights, quickly composed themselves. It was as if they were seeing two old friends after a long absence, their expressions a mix of familiarity and respect. The air around them felt charged with a sense of destiny, as if they had been preparing for this moment all along.

William, however, was visibly shaken. His eyes widened in shock, and his face paled as he stared at the spectral figures. The once confident guide now seemed small and vulnerable, caught off guard by the supernatural turn of events. He took a step back, his breath quickening, and a nervous sweat began to form on his brow. The presence of Sir Lancelot and Sir Percival, along with their ethereal glow, left him bewildered and frightened, his earlier bravado crumbling in the face of the unknown. "My apologies" said William, "I never meant any disrespect, I thought all of this was but a tale."

Sir Percival's expression softened slightly, though his gaze remained stern. "Stories are echoes of truth," he said. "You stand at a threshold, William Pendrick. But you are not yet ready."

William frowned. "Ready for what?"

Lancelot exchanged a glance with Percival before stepping forward. "You must be tested, just as the others were. Your trial is not of strength or sacrifice, it is one of patience, wisdom, and understanding. A warrior who acts without thought is no leader at all."

Before William could respond, the world around him shifted. The ruins of Tintagel Castle dissolved into a swirling mist, and the rusty sword in the stone vanished. The air grew still, and suddenly, there was nothing, no sound, no movement, no time.

He found himself standing in an endless void of pure white. There was nothing to see, nothing to hear, nothing to smell. The emptiness stretched infinitely in all directions, featureless and vast. A deep, resounding silence filled the space, pressing against him like an unseen force.

"Where am I?" William muttered.

"You are outside of time," Percival's voice echoed from nowhere and everywhere. "This will prepare you for your trial, young William. Sit. Breathe. Be still."

William clenched his fists. "What kind of trial is this? I thought I was supposed to prove myself!"

"You are," Lancelot's voice answered. "Now, sit."

Frustrated but with no other option, William lowered himself to the ground, crossing his legs. The silence pressed against him like a weight. He shifted uncomfortably. Minutes passed, or hours, he couldn't tell. The passage of time meant nothing in this place. His fingers twitched against his knees. He wanted to move, to do something.

"This is pointless," he muttered.

William Henry Belmont

"Is it?" Percival's voice drifted across the void. "You fidget. You resist. Why?"

William scowled. "Because nothing is happening!"

"You misunderstand," Lancelot's voice replied. "A true warrior does not simply act, he understands. A king must see clearly before he wields his sword. Do you know yourself, William Pendrick? Can you sit in silence and face what lies within?"

William gritted his teeth. His thoughts clawed at him, demanding distraction. His mind filled with doubt, *why me? I'm just a tour guide. I don't belong in some grand legend. I'm not special.*

But as the stillness stretched on, he began to realize something, this was his training. Not a battle, not a sacrifice. Just being. Accepting. Listening.

William inhaled slowly, feeling the cool air fill his lungs. The silence no longer felt oppressive. Before he knew it, he was no longer sitting in a white void but rather in a beautiful and serene open landscape, with a lake right in front of him.

The lake before him reflected his image, and for the first time, he truly looked at himself. *Who am I? What do I believe in? What do I stand for?*

Time passed. Maybe minutes. Maybe years. And then, from the fog along the lake, a figure emerged.

William stood, his breath passing in his throat. The man who approached was clad in regal armor, his presence commanding yet calm. His golden-brown hair was touched with silver, his eyes wise and knowing. The legendary King Arthur had arrived.

Arthur stopped at the lake's edge, his gaze steady. "You have finally stilled your mind," he said. "Only when the waters are calm can they reflect the truth. Now, tell me, William Pendrick, what does it mean to lead?"

William swallowed hard, his throat dry. The answer didn't come immediately. He thought of Isabella's determination, Akira's sacrifice, and his own doubts. He took a deep breath, letting his thoughts settle.

"To lead is not just to command," William said slowly. "It's to understand. To listen. To know when to act and when to wait. A true leader doesn't just wield power, they carry responsibility."

Arthur nodded, his eyes gleaming. "Good. And tell me, William, what is a friend?"

William hesitated. Then, as if the answer had always been there, he spoke. "A friend is someone who stands by you, even when they have nothing to gain. They are loyal not to your power, but to you. A leader without friends is a ruler, not a king."

Arthur's expression softened, approval clear in his gaze. "You have answered well. But one final truth remains. Excalibur does not choose a man by birthright alone; it chooses one worthy of the light. And now, William Pendrick, I give you my blessing."

The fog over the lake thickened, swirling like living mist. From the depths of the water, a slender, pale hand emerged, fingers delicately wrapped around the hilt of a magnificent sword. The Lady of the Lake, timeless and mystical, stepped forward, her gown flowing like liquid silver. She raised Excalibur from the water, its blade gleaming with pure, radiant light.

William's breath caught in his chest as she approached him, her gaze serene and knowing. She extended the sword to him, and with trembling hands, he took it. The moment his fingers wrapped around the hilt, a brilliant energy surged through him, warm and powerful.

Arthur smiled. "Excalibur has accepted you. Bear it well."

The world around him dissolved in a flash of golden light.

When William's vision cleared, he was back at Tintagel Castle, standing before Isabella and Akira. They stared at him in awe. He looked down at his hands. The rusted relic he had once dismissed as a mere prop was gone. In its place, the true Excalibur gleamed, its blade flawless and glowing with a divine radiance.

William Henry Belmont

As William stood before Isabella and Akira, the divine light of Excalibur continued to pulse gently in his hands. The sword began to hum, its brilliance flickering and shimmering, as if recognizing the shift in purpose. Slowly, the sword's solid form began to soften, the edges of the blade dissolving into delicate strands of light.

William watched as the hilt, still gleaming with a faint glow, transformed still in his hands. The sword began to coil like a ribbon, its golden hue fading into something more delicate, more personal. The sword curled and twisted gracefully into a small, elegant band.

In the blink of an eye, the band became a beautiful hair tie, its design simple yet noble, smooth and polished with a faint, shimmering diamond at its center, glowing with a subtle light. The hair tie, now a symbol of his strength and newfound wisdom, rested softly in William's hand.

He raised his hand, and with a look of resolve, William gently gathered his long hair. As he tied it back, the hair tie sat snugly in place, its light still pulsing gently. A perfect transformation: Excalibur, the legendary sword, now a symbol of wisdom and serenity, and his personal journey, woven into the strands of his own identity.

As the three heroes stood in quiet contemplation, their thoughts still swirling from the trials they had faced, a sudden presence filled the air. Warmth and weight seemed to press down on them, and with a midst of the golden light, King Arthur himself materialized, his regal form standing tall before them.

The heroes stood in awe as Arthur's piercing eyes met theirs, the weight of his gaze carrying the wisdom of centuries. His voice, calm but imbued with undeniable authority, rang out across time and space.

"You have proven yourselves worthy," he began, his words resonating deep within them. "The journey you have undertaken has tested your very souls, but your trials have not yet reached their end."

William, Isabella, and Akira exchanged glances, feeling a mixture of anticipation and uncertainty in their hearts. King Arthur continued, his voice growing more deliberate, as if carrying the weight of fate itself.

"You must now go and find your final companion," he instructed. "There is one who awaits for you, one whose presence will complete your circle. But to find them, you must first seek the place where wisdom is sacred, where knowledge and truth are honored above all else. You must go to the ancient city of thinkers. It is there that you will find the final piece of your journey, the one who holds the key to the future of your mission."

William, Isabella, and Akira nodded in unison, understanding the gravity of the quest before them. As King Arthur's form began to fade into the light, his last words echoed in their ears:

"The path ahead is challenging, but you are not alone. Trust in one another, and you will find your way."

With those final words, the light around them dimmed, leaving only the lingering warmth of King Arthur's presence. The three heroes stood together in silence, the next chapter of their journey now clear before them, their resolve strengthened by the legendary king's guidance.

Echoes of Legends

Part 5: The Tome Bearer

William Henry Belmont

As our heroes enter the city of thinkers, the weight of history hung in the air, but it wasn't just the grandeur of the ancient city that commanded their attention. There was something else, an almost tangible sense of purpose. They had come here for a reason, though the path ahead remained unclear.

"Where do we begin?" Isabella asked, her voice steady, though her eyes scanned the ancient city with a mix of wonder and curiosity.

The streets around them bustled with life, but there was something about the place that felt timeless, as though the whispers of ancient scholars still echoed through the air. A place of wisdom, of learning. William ran a hand through his hair.

"King Arthur said we would find our last companion here. But who? And where do we start?" William murmured.

They continued to move forward, making their way toward the steps that led up to a sacred temple, the city beneath them feeling smaller with each step. As they reached the top, near the temple's entrance, a cloaked figure stood in the shadows. Her presence was subtle, but it sent a chill through the air, something ancient and wise. As they approached, the figure turned to face them, her eyes sharp and knowing.

"I've been waiting for you," she said, his voice smooth, yet carrying the weight of centuries.

The cloaked figure moved with quiet confidence, leading the heroes deeper into the ruins of the ancient Parthenon. The crumbling columns and timeworn statues appeared around them, silent witnesses to centuries of wisdom and forgotten knowledge. Shadows flickered against the stone walls as shafts of sunlight filtered through the broken ceiling.

The heroes followed in a hushed mix of emotions, Isabella's curiosity burned bright, William's skepticism clashed with an undeniable sense of purpose, and Akira, ever the warrior, remained tense, prepared for the unknown. Their journey had brought them to this moment, and yet, none of them truly knew what awaited them in the heart of these ruins.

At last, the figure stopped in the center of the decayed temple, where the remnants of a once-grand altar stood beneath the open sky. She turned slowly to face them, her movements deliberate, measured. A lingering silence filled the air, thick with anticipation.

With a graceful motion, she lifted her hands to the hood of her cloak and slowly pulled it back. Long, sleek black hair, kissed with a hint of red, cascaded down her back, complemented her fair skin. Her sharp green eyes, striking and knowing, studied them with an intensity that sent a ripple through the group. She was effortlessly beautiful; she possesses delicate yet expressive features. But it was the depth in her gaze, the weight of wisdom, of history, that truly held them in place. She could not have been older than in her late twenties.

"Hello heroes, my name is Emeris, Helena Emeris" she said, her voice smooth yet carrying the weight of centuries.

The team of heroes stood in silence, exchanging uncertain glances. Helena's presence was both mesmerizing and unsettling, her words laced with a familiarity they did not understand.

"I am glad you have made it this far," she continued, her voice smooth and unwavering. Then, with a knowing smile, she added, "It is nice to see you again."

A spark of confusion passed between them. "Again?" William said, narrowing his eyes. Akira remained stoic, but Isabella, always the most curious, was the first to voice the question lingering in their minds.

"When have we met before?" she asked, her tone edged with both intrigue and suspicion.

Helena's smile deepened, as if she had been waiting for this very question. "I was behind your very first encounter with the magical world," she said, her emerald eyes locking onto Isabella's. "And every other event that has brought you closer to this moment."

Isabella's brow furrowed as she thought back. Her mind sifted through memories, piecing together the strange coincidences that had led her to this journey. The odd merchant who had placed the book in her hands. The mysterious shaman who had guided her to the hidden pyramid. The eccentric promoter who had given her the pamphlet that ultimately led her to Akira.

A shiver ran down her spine.

"You," Isabella breathed, eyes widening.

Helena nodded before she could finish. "Yes. I was all those people."

"How did you…" Isabella began, but Helena answered before she could finish. "The incantation of transfiguration," Helena said calmly, "not easily done."

A rush of emotions surged through Isabella, excitement, awe, and something else. Something colder. Distrust. She had been watched, guided, manipulated even. But why?

Before Isabella could press further, Helena continued.

"I needed you to gather the other heroes and their weapons," she said, her tone firm, the weight of command settling over her words. "There is a mission we must accomplish."

William, skeptical as ever, didn't hesitate. "Who are you," he demanded, "and what do you want with us?"

Helena let out a soft breath, as if she had anticipated his resistance. With a slow, deliberate motion, she drew back the edges of her cloak. Beneath the folds, her frame was slender and poised, but it was not her form that caught their attention, it was the tome she held in her left hand.

The book was ancient, bound in weathered leather, its cover engraved with symbols none of them could decipher. There was something unmistakably powerful about it, as though it pulsed with unseen energy.

"I understand your hesitation," Helena said, her voice as steady as ever. "Allow me to explain."

William Henry Belmont

Helena's gaze drifted past them for a moment, as if she were recalling a distant memory. When she spoke again, her voice was quieter, more introspective.

"Some time ago, I came to this very Parthenon, searching for something I could not name," she began. "A sense of belonging, a connection to the past, to my ancestors who once walked these halls. I had always felt... different, like I was meant for something greater, but I never knew what."

She took a slow breath before continuing.

"As I wandered through these ruins, I felt something calling to me, an energy unlike anything I had ever experienced. It was intoxicating, pulling me forward, guiding me, to the altar within the temple's heart."

Her fingers traced the worn edges of the tome in her hands.

"And there it was" she said, her voice barely above a whisper. "This book, resting atop the altar as if it had been waiting for me all along."

The three heroes listened in silence, the weight of her words settling over them.

"But the moment I touched it," Helena continued, her sharp green eyes darkening with memory, "a presence manifested before me. A ghostly apparition, yet more than just a specter. He was real, powerful, ancient. And I knew, even before he spoke, that I stood in the presence of legend."

She looked at them now, her expression unreadable.

"It was Merlin."

A stunned silence fell over the group.

'He told me the truth of my bloodline," Helena said, her voice steady but laced with an emotion none of them could quite place. "That I was his heir, long lost to time. And with that truth came a duty, to guide those who would stand against the heir of Morgana Le Fay."

Her gaze swept over them, measuring their reactions.

"That is why I brought you here. Why I have been watching you. The time has come.

Just like our ancestors stopped Morgana, now it is time for us to stop her heir."

Helena let a small smile form at the corner of her lips as she observed the three heroes before her. They had come far, each mastering their own journey, but now the real challenge would begin.

"Now that you are all here, with your weapons in hand," she said. "You must train, not as individuals, but as a unit. Only together will you be able to stand against Luca's darkness."

Before any of them could respond, Helena raised her hand, and the air around them shimmered. The ancient ruins blurred, the stone pillars dissolving into light, and within moments, they found themselves standing in a vast open field. The grass stretched endlessly before them, vibrant green against the backdrop of a dense forest. The wind carried the scent of earth and fresh leaves, untouched and wild. The sky above was open and endless.

The three heroes turned in awe, taking in their surroundings.

Without hesitation, they reached for their relics. The air whooshed with energy as Isabella's pendant flared to life, transforming into her mighty axe. Akira's bracelet gleamed like the moon, his lance forming in his grip. William's hair tie burned with golden light, reshaping into the legendary blade he now wielded with growing familiarity.

Helena watched them with an approving nod.

"Isabella," she called, her tone carrying authority, "you will lead this group."

Isabella turned to her, eyes widening slightly. "Me?"

"You are strong, determined, and willing to do what is necessary," Helena said. "You have the heart of a leader."

Isabella swallowed, glancing at Akira and William. They nodded, accepting Helena's words without argument.

Helena's gaze shifted to Akira. "Your strength lies in movement, in precision. You must learn how to attack as one with your allies, strike where they create openings, and create opportunities for them in turn. Do not fight alone. Use your speed to guide the battlefield."

"I think I can manage that." Akira said, as he gave Isabella a smile.

Finally, Helena turned to William. "And you," Her voice softened, but there was no less weight in her words. "You must let go of your doubts. Your strength is not in leading, but in supporting. You are the resin that bonds the team together, the light that allows the team to see. Trust them and trust yourself."

William clenched his jaw but nodded. He had never seen himself as a warrior, let alone part of some destined battle, but something about Helena's words resonated deep within him.

Helena extended her hands. The air around them grew densely with magic as the wind howled, and from the swirling energy, monstrous forms began to take shape. Shadows twisted into towering creatures with scaled hides and burning eyes, dragon-like beasts from another realm. Their claws dug into the earth as they let out deafening roars, wings unfurling with a rush of air.

The heroes tensed, weapons raised.

Isabella was the first to charge. Her axe pulsed with power as she swung at the nearest beast, sending shockwaves through the ground. The creature staggered but remained standing. Akira dashed past her, his lance slicing through the air with precision, forcing another beast to recoil. William stood his ground, waiting for the right moment before striking, his blade glowing with golden light as he deflected an incoming attack.

But as fierce as they fought, the beasts adapted, striking back with greater force. One by one, the heroes were knocked back.

"Akira, you have Sir Lancelot speed, you need to give me an opening to attack." Isabella commanded instead of explaining.

William Henry Belmont

Akira did not answer, he stood tall in silence but clearly annoyed.

"William, what are you even doing," Isabella demanded, "you have Excalibur, do you mind helping out."

"What did I do?" William asked, slightly confused in a childish manner.

Helena watched impassively. "You fight well," she said. "But you fight as individuals. Let's try again."

They exchanged glances before regrouping.

"You are not doing what I am telling you to do Akira" Isabella snapped at him.

Akira turned, jaw tighten, "I am not your servant for you to order around, Bella."

"That is not how I meant it and you know it" Isabella replied to Akira.

Helena clapped her hands as to get their attention, "Enough. Both of you." Helena looked at Akira and then at Isabella, "apologize."

Isabella crossed her arms, "I am not going to apologize to him."

Akira scoffed and mimicked, "'I am not going to apologize to him.'" clearly mocking her, intending on making her even more angry.

"Ugh," Isabella puffed, stamping her foot on the ground once, before rolling her eyes and walking away in a small, unmistakable tantrum.

Helena's eyes snapped at him. "Really, Akira, really?"

Akira straightened at once.

Helena sighed, rubbing her temples. "This attitude will not win the fight against Morgana's heir. Either learn to fight together or you will die together."

Both Isabella and Akira took a deep breath and remembered why the team is training together.

"let's continue our training, this time, together," Isabella commanded.

Akira nodded. "I'll create an opening." Isabella then turned to William, "William, you back Akira. I, go for the finish."

"Let us start with just one beast this time." Helena said, waving her hand as a dragon-like creature materialized before them.

The battle began again. Akira moved first, his lance glowing with the combined force of wind and water, striking fast and pushing the beast off balance. William followed immediately, sending a burst of light from Excalibur that blinded the creature, giving Isabella the perfect chance to land a crushing blow with the weight of earth and stone. The beast collapsed, dissolving into mist.

Helena smiled. "Better. Again."

They repeated their attacks, refining their teamwork, learning to flow as one. Helena guided them, teaching them to channel the true power of their weapons. Isabella's axe, wielding the force of earth itself, capable of shattering the ground beneath her enemies; Akira's lance, commanding the speed of wind and the fluidity of water, striking in rapid, unpredictable patterns; and William's sword, a beacon of pure light, shielding his allies and cutting through darkness itself.

With each battle, their movements became sharper, their trust in one another growing.

Finally, as the last beast faded into nothingness, Helena lowered her hands, ending the trial.

"You have made progress," she said, her voice steady. "Akira, William, continue training." Helena turned to Isabella, her tone leaving no room for argument, "Walk with me"

Isabella follows Helena deep into the forest that surrounded their training grounds. Uncertain of what Helena will teach her, but certainly, it would not be easy.

After what it felt like an eternity of relentless training, days and nights blended. Helena finally stepped forward, her sharp green eyes scanning the three heroes with quiet approval. The wind rustled through the grass, carrying the weight of the moment.

"We are ready," she declared, her voice steady, yet filled with the gravity of what was to come.

The heroes straightened, gripping their weapons. Though their bodies were sore, their spirits burned with determination.

Helena continued, "Now, it is time for you to step onto the battlefield where it all began, the sacred ground where King Arthur and the Knights of the Round Table stood against Morgana's darkness."

A hush fell over the group as the significance of her words settled in. Isabella, Akira, and William exchanged glances. They had heard the legends, but to stand in the very place where history had been written… it was both thrilling and daunting.

"But understand this," Helena said, her gaze darkening. "Once you set foot upon that land, Luca will sense our presence. He is the heir to Morgana's legacy, and like her, he will not let this battle end until he has claimed victory."

Akira clenched his jaw. "So, he'll come to finish what she started."

Helena nodded. "Yes. And this time, it will be us who must stand against evil."

William exhaled slowly, gripping the hilt of his sword. "Then we'd better make sure we're ready for him."

A small, knowing smile crossed Helena's lips. "Our training is over. What come next is not a test, it is the battle that will decide the fate of our world."

All the heroes nodded at her, letting her know they were ready.

With that, she raised her hands, magic crackling around her fingertips. The air grew thick with energy as the world around them began to shift, the familiar green plains dissolving into shimmering light. The battle that would decide the fate of their world was about to begin.

The heroes now stood at the edge of a vast open plain, near an enchanted forest. With a smooth movement of her hand, Helena conjured a small fire "We need to rest,"

William Henry Belmont

Helena said, "tomorrow, Morgana's heir will feel our presence here, and the battle will begin."

Our four heroes lay upon the ground, exhausted. Helena and William fell asleep almost at once. Akira lays on his back, arms crossed beneath his head, gazing at the stars, his thoughts drifting towards the future.

Isabella could not sleep.

She rose quietly and sat on a nearby rock, eyes fixed on the dark horizon, her thoughts lingering on the battle awaiting beyond the night. After a moment, she turned, believing Akira was already sleeping. But instead, she found him watching her. The look he gave her made her exhale softly.

"let's take a walk," Akira said, "maybe that will help us find our sleep"

They moved away from the fire, into the trees, where the night grew deeper and quieter. Time passed unnoticed, measured only by their steps and shared silence, their company made them feel as if time move faster. They finally stopped beneath an old weeping tree, its branches moving softly with the wind. Moonlight filtered through its branches, casting silver streaks of light.

Akira stepped closer. Isabella did not move away.

They took each other's hands, their eyes locked together.

Isabella's gaze drifted past Akira's shoulder.

Just beyond them, near the base of a stone worn smooth by time, leaves and small wildflowers had gathered naturally along the rock's surface. Rain and wind had pressed them together into a quiet shape, imperfect yet pure, unplanned, unmistakable. A heart, formed without intention, resting there as if the forest itself had paused to leave something behind. Just for them.

Isabella felt her heart skip a beat.

Akira followed her eyes and saw it too. For a moment, neither of them spoke. The vastness of the beautiful landscape paled in comparison to Isabella's natural beauty.

William Henry Belmont

The long road that had led them here, all of it seemed to fade, leaving only that small, fragile symbol between them.

They held each other's hands with a new sensation between them. Their eyes met as they never had before. Slowly, they began to sway, guided by the rhythm of the wind rustling through the weeping tree's branches.

♪ Akira: All my life, I have walked without a purpose set. But then I saw you, I felt it inside, my purpose is now clear.

Isabella: The battle, before us, has no promise of mercy. Yet when you stand, beside me, I feel we can win, I feel hope reminds.

Akira: It doesn't matter, what tomorrow, may have in store for us. What I am I give, what I am is yours. I will be your shield.

Isabella: I was taught, to stand alone, to endure without fear, to need nothing more. But now, I understand, that needing you is, a beautiful thing, now please hold me close, to you mi amor. ♪

At that moment, Akira felt like the luckiest man alive.

Isabella drew him nearer.

Their lips met, gently, carrying everything that did not need to be spoken.

Echoes of Legends

Part 6: The Battle for the Fate of the World

William Henry Belmont

As the morning took over the vast plain, the air crackled with tension as the four heroes stood in the heart of the vast, desolate valley. Above them, the sky shook with storm-blackened clouds, swirling as if summoned by an ancient and vengeful force. The ground beneath their feet trembled, pulsing with an ominous energy that seemed to whisper of impending doom. A chilling wind howled through the valley, carrying the scent of rain and something darker, something unnatural.

Isabella tightened her grip on Percival's axe, its weight grounding her as the blade pulsed with the raw power of earth, a faint, golden glow tracing its intricate carvings. Beside her, Akira spun Lancelot's lance effortlessly in his hand, the weapon gleaming like a fragment of the moon, its light a defiant contrast against the growing darkness. William stood resolute, Excalibur firm in his grasp, its hilt warm with divine energy, the blade humming with a celestial radiance that cut through the gloom. At his side, Helena clutched Merlin's tome, her fingers gliding over its ancient text as she whispered an incantation under her breath, her eyes fixed on the figure emerging from the distance.

Luca, who had teleported suddenly from nowhere, stepped forward, his dark robes flowing as if alive. The unnatural violet glow of his eyes burned with malice, and in his grasp, Morgana's staff full of dark power. A smirk spread across his lips as his voice slithered through the valley, thick with condescension and amusement.

"So," he mused, his tone dripping with mockery, "the descendants of Arthur's court have come to challenge me." His fingers tightened around the staff. "How utterly foolish."

Isabella, looking at Luca dead in the eyes and says, "why are you doing this, you don't have to."

Luca smirked, tilting his head as if amused by the question. He takes a slow step forward. "The world aches under the weight of fools, longing, whether they admit it or

not, for a leader worthy of their loyalty.
And who better than I? Luca, last living
link to Morgana La fey, heir to her legacy
of power and purpose."

Isabella stepped forward.

"You are wrong," she said.

Luca did not flinch. A faint smile
touched his lips. "Keep telling yourself
that."

William shook his head. "People will
never serve you."

"They already do," Luca replied calmly.
"They simply have not admitted it yet."

Akira's voice cut through the air. "No.
Not while I still breathe."

Luca sized Akira up and down, a slow
smile forming on his lips. "I can change
that."

Helena stepped closer, her jaw tight.
"Your arrogance blinds you."

"And your wisdom stops where mine
begins," Luca answered without hesitation.

Isabella's hands trembled at her sides.
"No… you are wrong."

Luca's fingers tightened around Morgana's staff, creaking beneath his grip. "I am the only one who can rule this world."

Isabella raised her axe, knuckles white. "Hate will never win. Not while we still stand."

"Unlike you," Luca said, his voice sharpening, "I am willing to do what it takes."

"A victory without purity is no victory at all," Isabella replied.

Luca shifted his stance, just enough to promise violence. "Then you are weaker than I thought."

Akira stepped between them, planting himself firmly in Luca's path. With the strength only a man who understood what needed to be protected, Akira said, "Don't you dare."

Akira advanced a single step. "If you move, you die where you stand."

Luca laughed softly, almost pleased. "Yes… I like that attitude."

His gaze slid to Helena. "Merlin's hatred for Morgana blinded him," he said, gesturing to the scarred land around them. "Look around. Under my rule, it will be better."

"Do not speak his name," Helena snapped, before continuing,

"There must be another way. You do not understand what is right." Helena continued.

"Do not project your fear and borrowed wisdom onto me," Luca replied.

Helena raised her tome, light gathering along its edges. "I will not listen to one so corrupted."

Isabella stepped forward again. There was no argument left in her eyes now. She looked at Akira, and he met her gaze, nodding once. A nod of love, of trust, of acceptance.

She turned back to Luca. "So be it. It ends today."

Luca smiled.

"You may try."

A low chuckle rumbled from Luca's chest, dark and cruel. The storm above roared in response, and the valley trembled as the battle began.

The battlefield erupted in a clash of light and darkness, a storm of raw power shaking the valley to its core. Akira lunged first, his lance a streak of silver as he struck with relentless precision, each movement swift and deadly. But Luca, raising his hand, conjured a wall of swirling shadows coiled around him, absorbing Akira's blows with effortless ease.

Helena followed immediately, whispering an incantation as a surge of arcane fire burst from her hand, roaring toward Luca like a wrathful inferno. He leapt back, the flames licking at the edges of his robes, forcing him to retreat. Before he could regain his footing, William charged forward, Excalibur blazing like the dawn itself. The sacred blade clashed against Luca's dark magic with a deafening explosion, sending ripples of energy surging through the battlefield.

Isabella joined the fight, her axe cleaving through the air with brutal force, the power of the earth pulsing through every strike. But Luca was quick, his form weaving between attacks with inhuman grace, his dark magic twisting into writhing tendrils that lashed out at the heroes. The tendrils struck with crushing force, hurling them backward like ragdolls.

With a flick of his wrist, Luca summoned a spear of pure shadow, its form jagged and pulsing with malevolent energy. A wicked grin curled on his lips as he hurled it straight toward Isabella, the weapon cutting through the air like a death sentence.

Isabella closed her eyes tightly, bracing herself for the blow that would end her life. The moments stretched unbearably, but the strike never came. Trembling, she dared to open her eyes, her vision blurred by the tears that rolled down her rosy cheeks. Her breath fastened as she took in the sight before her: Akira stood between her and her attacker; the cruel spear buried deep in his chest.

He had thrown himself into harm's way for her.

"Akira, no…" she whispered, her voice breaking as she reached out to steady him. His legs weakened, and she caught him by the waist, his arms weakly finding their way around her shoulders. As his strength dwindled away, he sank to his knees, pulling Isabella down with him. She cradled him in her arms, her tears now falling freely onto his face.

Their eyes Locked, a clash of emotions conveyed in a silent exchange. Pain tore through Isabella's heart like a storm, while Akira's gaze was steady, submersed with a quiet, unwavering hope. He had done the only thing he knew to be true, the only thing that mattered. He had given his life to protect hers.

His breaths grew shallower, and his body became heavier in her embrace. "Akira, please…" she choked, her voice trembling with desperation. His lips parted, as though he wanted to say something, but no words came. His eyes slowly closed, the light within them dimming as he succumbed to eternal rest.

With a trembling hand, Isabella cupped his face, her thumb brushing gently against his cheek. She leaned forward, pressing a solemn, tender kiss to his lips, a kiss that spoke of all the unspoken words, gratitude, love, and sorrow. It was her final way of telling him what he meant to her, her silent promise to carry his sacrifice in her heart forever.

Luca's laughter echoed across the battlefield, cold and maniacal. Though he had failed to kill Isabella, the act of ending Akira's life filled him with an intoxicating sense of triumph. His eyes gleamed with sadistic pleasure as he rejoiced in his dark victory.

From the distance, William charged forward, Excalibur shining brilliantly in his grasp. He aimed to cut down the twisted figure before him. But Luca, ever watchful, sidestepped effortlessly. With a flick of his staff, he unleashed a surge of dark magic that sent William hurtling backward, his body crashing against the ground with a forceful thud.

Helena stood at the edge of the battlefield; her gaze locked on Luca with a fiery intensity. The grin on Luca's face faded, replaced by a distrustful scowl. She gripped Merlin's tome tightly, her knuckles white with determination, and closed her eyes, whispering an incantation under her breath.

Helena looks at Akira's body. For a moment, she says nothing. Then her breath caught, "No…"

The word barely left her lips before it shattered into something else entirely.

"AHHHHHHHHHH"

The cry tore from Helena's chest, not as grief, but as defiance made sound. The ground beneath her feet fractures as her power answers.

Light surges upwards in violent waves, raw and blinding, forcing the air itself to recoil. Her body locked in place, as something ancient and unrestrained broke free within her.

This is no incantation, no discipline, it was power unleashed.

Her hair lifted as if pulled by an unseen force. The air bent, the ground beneath her feet cracked, unable to hold what was being released.

"You will pay for this Luca." Helena says in a menacing voice.

Luca's triumphant posture stiffened as he sensed a sudden shift. Whipping around, he found Helena standing impossibly close, her eyes blazing with resolve. She had teleported behind him in an instant. Luca let out a furious scream, raising his staff to unleash a torrent of dark energy. Helena countered, her white magic forming a radiant shield that deflected his attack effortlessly.

Their duel began in earnest, magic clashing in a dazzling display of light and shadow. White and dark energy collided in rapid succession, the air around them snapped with raw power. Neither could gain the upper hand, their abilities so evenly matched that their battle became a violent stalemate.

As Luca focused his full attention on Helena, William seized the opportunity to strike again. Excalibur glowed brighter than ever, its energy seemingly resonating with William's unshakable determination. He leapt forward; sword poised for a decisive blow. But Luca, sensing the movement, let out a deep laugh that chilled the air.

Luca's hunger for power and victory was absolute.

With a flick of his free hand, Luca conjured another spear of dark magic and hurled it mid-air. The spear struck William with brutal precision, his lifeless body fell to the ground. Helena screamed in anguish, her voice echoing with both fury and despair.

Luca's smile returned, more sinister than before. He turned his attention back to Helena, who was now desperately channeling her remaining power to defend herself. With a ruthless gesture, Luca pointed at Helena's tome, yanking her tome from her grasp with a burst of dark energy. The sacred artifact flew into his hand, and he held it alongside his staff, both instruments of immense power now under his control.

"You were never a match for me," Luca mocked, his voice dripping with malice.

Concentrating his magic, Luca combined the energies of both the staff and tome, forming a devastating force that surged toward Helena like a meteor of pure destruction. She stood tall, her face calm despite the inevitable. Closing her eyes, she accepted her fate, she whispers to herself, hands together as in prayer, as she waits for the strike. The dark magic struck her with a deafening roar, obliterating her completely, leaving no trace behind.

From the distance, Isabella remained frozen, still cradling Akira's lifeless body. Tears streamed down her face as she watched in horror, unable to look away. Her heart shattered further with each death, her despair now an unbearable weight.

Luca turned toward her, his malevolent gaze locking with hers. He stood as a god of destruction, his staff in one hand and Helena's tome in the other, radiating an aura of absolute power. His triumphant expression made it clear; he had won.

Isabella, her strength fading and her hope flickering, bowed her head. Her trembling hands came together, and she began to whisper a desperate incantation. She called upon the magic Helena had taught her, her voice steadying as her will solidified. The air around her shimmered with faint light as her power gathered.

As she channeled her magic, a sudden light erupted from the weapons of her fallen comrades. Excalibur, still clutched in William's lifeless hand, pulsed with golden radiance, while Akira's lance, stained with his sacrifice, gleamed like silver moonlight. The two weapons trembled, their forms dissolving into pure energy before merging into twin spheres of light. With a burst of speed, they rushed toward Isabella, their glow intensifying as they reached her hands, filling her with newfound strength.

In one final act of defiance, Isabella conjured a spell. A brilliant glow enveloped her, and in an instant, she vanished from the battlefield, leaving Luca alone in his cruel victory.

As Luca stood among the shattered remains of the fallen heroes, savoring his victory, a faint, haunting sound reached his ears, a baby's cry; soft yet piercing, drifting through the air like an echo from future time.

Part 7: A New World

William Henry Belmont

Twenty years had passed since their defeat. The world had changed under Luca's rule, shaped by his vision of power and control. But Isabella had long since removed herself from it. Now in her early forties, she remained as striking as ever, though time had carved its traces upon her; lines of sorrow, memories of battles lost. She lived in seclusion, deep within an ancient forest, far from the reach of Luca's dominion.

The fire crackled softly as she stirred a pot over the fireplace, the scent of herbs and simmering broth filling the small hut. It was a simple life, quiet and undisturbed, just as she wanted.

Then came the knock.

A single, firm drum against the wooden door. Isabella stood still, her grip tightening around the wooden spoon. She knew that knock. With a weary sigh, she set the spoon down and moved to the door, opening it to reveal a cloaked figure standing in the dim light. Underneath the hood, a familiar face.

"I told you time and time again," Isabella said, crossing her arms, her voice edged with exasperation. "Neither you nor I are training him. We lost. Accept it."

Helena, standing in the doorway, did not flinch. She was as beautiful as before but a shadow of the same. Her piercing eyes held steady, unwavering in their resolve. "He is our last hope," she said. "The son of two heroes. You must understand."

Isabella's jaw tightened. She had heard this plea before, too many times. The same argument, the same desperate insistence that the fight wasn't over. She turned away, retreating inside.

"I said no," she muttered, her voice colder now. "It doesn't matter how many times over the years you ask."

Helena exhaled, a slow, measured breath. For a moment, it seemed like she might argue, but instead, she simply pulled her hood back over her head.

William Henry Belmont

"Then I will ask again next year," she said softly before stepping away into the night. "One day, he will know who he is, not by my hand or yours."

Isabella watched her go, her expression unreadable. Then, with a heavy sigh, she closed the door, locking it behind her.

"Who was that, Mom?" asked Ulisses, his voice calm but curious. He stood near the doorway, watching Isabella with his ever-slanted eyes. His brown skin, kissed by years under the sun, bore the same warm undertones as his mother's, and though lean, his muscles were defined, shaped by a life of work and survival.

"Nobody," Isabella said quickly, her tone sharper than she intended. She didn't meet his gaze. "I told you before, just an old friend. But she had to go."

Ulisses studied her for a moment, sensing the tension in her shoulders. He had long learned not to push when she was like this.

"Go gather some firewood," Isabella continued, her voice softening just a little. "We need to prepare dinner."

With a nod, Ulisses grabbed his small axe and stepped outside, letting the door shut behind him. The evening air was cool against his skin as he ventured deeper into the woods. He had walked these paths since childhood, he knew every tree, every root, every hidden trail. Yet, as he moved through the familiar landscape, something felt… off.

Then, he saw it.

A narrow path, winding between the trees, one he had never noticed before. That didn't make sense. He had roamed this forest for nearly twenty years. He knew every inch of it. And yet, this trail stretched before him, as if it had always been there, waiting to be seen.

Curiosity tugged at him. Without thinking, he followed the path, stepping carefully over the roots and under low, hanging branches. It led him to the mouth of a small cave, half-hidden by thick foliage.

A strange hum filled the air. Faint at first, like the distant ringing of a chime, but as he stepped inside, it grew stronger.

Then, movement.

Two small orbs of light hovered just above the cave floor, dim, almost imperceptible. Yet, as Ulisses drew closer, they pulsed. The glow intensified, shifting from a soft ember to a deep, molten red. Heat radiated from them, sending shivers up his arms.

Before he could react, the lights surged forward, twisting and reshaping midair. In an instant, they were no longer mere orbs but objects. One, a bracelet of silver metal, its surface etched with intricate blue engravings; the other, a hair tie, its deep golden hue shimmering unnaturally.

They hovered for a heartbeat before shooting toward him. His hands instinctively rose, catching them out of the air.

The warmth of the objects settled into his skin, a strange, electric energy coursing through his fingers. He didn't know what they were. But somehow, deep in his bones, he knew they had been waiting for him.

With his arms full of firewood, Ulises returned to his mother, his expression unreadable. The weight of what he had discovered pressed against his palms as he stepped into the warm glow of their small hut.

"I found these in the forest," he said, extending his hands to her. The firelight flickered over the strange relics, one a silver, engraved bracelet, the other a deep golden hair tie.

Isabella turned, her gaze falling on his outstretched hands. The moment she saw them, her breath felt stilled. Her fingers curled slightly, as if she had been struck by an invisible force. For a long moment, she said nothing. Then, with a heavy sigh, she slowly sat down by the fire, her eyes dark with something between sorrow and resignation.

William Henry Belmont

"I never wanted you to find those," she murmured. "I hid them well, from you and from Helena."

Ulisses frowned, confused by his mother's wavering voice. He had never seen his mother like this before. She was always strong, always composed. But now, there was something fragile in her demeanor, as if she were standing at the edge of a long and buried grief.

"Mom… can you please tell me the truth?" he asked, his voice steady but gentle.

Isabella hesitated. Her hands clenched into fists, then relaxed. Finally, she lifted her gaze to meet his eyes.

"The bracelet belonged to your father," she said at last, her voice barely above a whisper. "And the hair tie… it belonged to a dear friend of mine."

Ulisses remained silent, waiting.

Taking a slow, steady breath, Isabella began.

She told him everything. How she had once been a warrior, not just a mother living in seclusion. How she had discovered that she was a descendant of Sir Percival, one of the knights of the Round Table. How she had set out on a quest, searching for others like her, bound by blood to legends long past. She spoke of William, the heir to Arthur himself, and Akira, his father, the last descendant of Sir Lancelot.

She told him of their battle against Luca, the one they had lost.

But more than that, she spoke of love and loss. Of how she had fought beside the man who would become the love of her life, his father. How they had stood together in their final battle, knowing the odds were against them. And how, in the end, she had lost him.

"I lost him that day," she whispered, staring into the flames. "I lost all of them. And with them, I lost my hope."

The room was silent except for the crackling fire. Ulisses stood there, the weight of her words pressing down on him like an invisible force. He looked at the

William Henry Belmont

relics in his hands, the last remnants of a story long buried.

Ulisses, understandably confused by the weight of his mother's revelations, tightened his grip on the relics in his hands. His mind raced, trying to piece together the truth he had been denied his entire life. "But Mom," he said, his voice firm despite the storm of emotions inside him, "if there's a way to defeat Lord Luca, we should take it."

Isabella lowered her head, sorrow drawn into every line of her face. The firelight cast flickering shadows across the small hut, but the heaviness in her chest was darker still. She had buried this part of her life for so long, hoping it would never resurface.

Ulisses took a step forward, determination burning in his eyes. "You can train me," he insisted, his voice steady. "Show me how to fight. I will defeat him."

Isabella exhaled sharply, as if his words had struck a wound that had never fully healed. She looked up at her son, so young, so full of the same reckless courage that had once driven her, William, and Akira and Helena forward. And just like them, he didn't yet understand the cost of war.

"You don't know what you're saying," she said finally, her voice laced with pain. "You don't know what it means to lose everything."

"You don't understand," Isabella said, her voice heavy with years of grief. She turned away from Ulisses, as if avoiding looking at her own reflection in him, so full of fire, so desperate to fight was too much to bear. "That day, I lost your father. And I will not lose you too."

Ulisses furrowed his brow, his hands tightening into fists at his sides. "But Mother"

She held up a hand, silencing him before he could argue. Her gaze lifted to the dim glow of the fire, as though seeing something far beyond it, something only she could remember. "I don't care if Lord Luca rules over this world," she said finally, her voice quiet but unyielding. "The stars

William Henry Belmont

do not seem any dimmer if you never look up at the sky."

Ulisses stepped back, stunned by her words. "So, you would rather live in hiding forever? Pretending none of this matter?"

"Yes," Isabella whispered. "If it means not losing you."

The room fell into silence, thick with unspoken emotions. Ulisses could feel the weight of her sorrow pressing down on him, but something inside him refused to yield. He had spent his life in this quiet seclusion, but he had always sensed that there was more to his mother, more to himself, more to the world beyond the trees.

And now, the truth stood before him, undeniable.

Isabella exhaled a slow, weary sigh. "Open the door, Ulisses. Tell her she can come inside."

Ulisses hesitated, glancing toward the entrance. No one had knocked, no shadow loomed beyond the threshold. But something in his mother's tone made him obey without question. He walked to the door, unlatched it, and pulled it open.

Helena was already there, standing in the dim light of dusk, waiting.

She met his gaze with a quiet understanding before stepping inside. The fire flickered, casting long shadows across the room. As she entered, her eyes met Isabella's, years of history, of unspoken grief, of the battle fought and lost, passing between them in a single glance. There was no need for words. They both knew the pain that had followed in the wake of Luca's triumph.

Isabella gestured toward a chair by the fire, and Helena sat without hesitation. The only sound between them for a long moment was the crackling of burning wood, filling the silence with its restless murmurs.

At last, Isabella spoke. "If we are going to train Ulisses… it can't be like last time. Something has to change. I will not let my son walk the same path as his father."

William Henry Belmont

Helena nodded solemnly. "I understand." She straightened in her seat, her fingers resting lightly on her lap. "Even though I lost Merlin's Tome, I haven't stopped training. I have spent my time in meditation, searching for another way."

Isabella studied her, waiting.

Helena inhaled deeply, then continued. "The legendary weapons, the relics, the Lance of Lancelot and Excalibur, they are more than just tools of war. Their power is fluid, waiting to be shaped by the will of their wielder." She leaned forward slightly, her voice carrying the weight of revelation. "With the right guidance, Ulisses won't need to wield them as mere weapons. They can become an armor and a shield, something to protect rather than destroy."

Isabella's expression was unreadable, but the firelight caught something in her eyes, a flicker of hope, and perhaps fear.

"You're certain?" she asked.

Helena held her gaze. "I would not be here if I wasn't."

A heavy silence settled between them once more, filled with the ghosts of old regrets and the fragile hope of something new.

Ulisses met his mother's gaze, his eyes burning with conviction. "Mother, I can do this. I know it."

Isabella studied him, searching his face for any hint of doubt, but there was none. In him, she saw his father's unwavering determination, the same unshakable resolve that had made her fall in love with Akira. And beneath that, she saw her own fire, the same eagerness that had once driven her to fight, to carve her place in the world.

She glanced at Helena, then back at her son, her mind racing. Was this truly the right path? Could she bear to watch him walk into the fire that had scarred her?

She took a slow, measured breath. There was no escape from fate.

"So be it," she said at last, looking at her son, her voice steady. "Your godmother and I will train you."

William Henry Belmont

Helena's breath quickens, her chest rising as if she had been holding hope at bay for too long. Ulisses clenched his fists, his muscles tensing with anticipation, the weight of his destiny settling onto his shoulders, Isabella, however, felt only the aching pull of worry. She had made her decision, but her heart refused to quiet its fears.

Part 8: The Sanctuary of Echoes

William Henry Belmont

Helena looks at both Isabella and Ulisses, her expression calm yet filled with purpose. She gestures for them to stand.

"Take out your relics," she says.

Ulisses reaches into his pockets and carefully pulls out the bracelet and hair tie, small, humble objects that contain immeasurable power. He holds them out for Helena to see. Isabella, without a word, moves her hair aside and pulls down her shirt collar just enough to reveal the pendant resting against her skin. She had never taken it off.

Helena studies them both, a soft smile forming on her lips. "Good," she murmurs. Then, with a wave of her hand, the relics begin to glow.

Their light is blinding, filling the room with a brilliance so intense that Ulisses instinctively shuts his eyes. The energy hums through the air, crackling like a storm contained within a single moment. When the glow begins to fade, and the three of them slowly open their eyes, they find themselves standing somewhere else entirely.

Gone is Isabella's hut.

Instead, they are in an ancient, tranquil land bathed in moonlight. The night sky stretches endlessly above them, littered with stars so vivid they seem to pulse with life. A river winds through the open plain, its waters shimmering silver beneath the glow of the full moon. Tall grass sways in a gentle breeze, and in the distance, trees stand like silent guardians, their leaves whispering secrets of forgotten times.

Ulisses spins around, taking it all in, his excitement evident. "Where… what is this place?"

Helena steps forward, her voice even, almost reverent. "This place exists only within the relics. It is a realm outside of time, created by those who came before us. Here, you can train for as long as you need, and not a single moment will pass in the real world. And more than that, time does not touch you here. You will not age, not until you leave."

Ulisses' eyes widen, his mind racing with the possibilities. An endless training ground. A chance to grow stronger without losing time. He can do this. He must do this.

But then he looks at his mother.

His excitement vanishes.

Isabella is staring at him, but not with her usual warmth. Her eyes are hard, focused, intense in a way he has never seen before. There is no softness in her face, no reassurance, no comfort. Instead, there is determination, steel, and a flicker of something else. Anger.

When she finally speaks, her voice is sharp and unwavering.

"Your father was a world champion. I was a renowned boxer. And still, we lost to Luca," she says, her words cutting through the night like a blade. "You don't stand a chance. You have never trained for a single day in your life. That changes now. Your physical training starts as soon as the sun rises."

Ulisses swallows, his muscles tensing. He has never heard her speak to him like this. Never seen her look at him with such raw intensity.

Then Helena steps forward, her voice softer but no less firm.

"And your mind," she adds, "has never been trained either. Your body is nothing without focus. You will learn to meditate, to still your thoughts, to sharpen your will. The relics are not mere tools, Ulisses. They are extensions of your very soul. As you are now, they will never listen to you."

The wind shifts, rustling the grass.

Ulisses clenches his fists. He has no words, only the quiet, unshakable realization that this will not be easy.

But he wouldn't have it any other way.

As the first light of dawn stretches across the sky, the sun's golden rays touch Ulisses' face, stirring him awake. His body aches with anticipation, his muscles stiff from the previous day, but before he can

William Henry Belmont

even fully register he is awake, a shadow looms over him.

Isabella stands in front of him, arms crossed, her expression harden.

"Get up," she commands.

Ulisses bolts upright, his heart pounding. There is no warmth in her voice, only cold resolve. He meets her gaze, but there is no room for hesitation.

Isabella lifts her hand and points toward the horizon. "Do you see that tree over there?"

Ulisses squints, following her finger. It takes him a moment to spot it, a solitary tree standing impossibly far away, so distant that it looks no larger than his thumb.

"Yes, Mother."

"Then run to it, touch it, and run back," she says flatly. "You have one hour."

Ulisses' stomach tightens. His breath catches in his throat. The distance is immense, more than he has ever run in his life. He glances at his mother, hoping for some sign that she's exaggerating, that she might soften the command.

But her expression remains hard as stone.

He knows better than to complain.

"Yes, Mother."

Without another word, he takes off.

The ground is firm beneath his feet, the cool morning air rushing past him as he sprints forward. The rhythmic pounding of his footsteps fills his ears, his heartbeat quickens. At first, it feels exhilarating, the wind against his face, the freedom of movement. But soon, the excitement fades, replaced by the burn in his legs, the tightness in his chest.

The tree, still so far away.

Each step feels heavier, the distance stretching endlessly before him. He forces himself to push forward, gasping for breath as sweat beads down his face. Finally, after what feels like an eternity, his hand slaps against the rough bark of the tree.

No time to rest.

William Henry Belmont

He turns and forces himself back the way he came. His legs scream in protest, his lungs raw as he drags-in air. His vision blurs, his body feels like lead, but he keeps going, because he has no choice.

When he finally stumbles back to his mother, he collapses to his knees, hands pressed to the earth as he fights for breath. His entire body trembles, every muscle burning, his heart hammering against his ribs.

But Isabella does not kneel to comfort him.

She does not praise him.

"Get, up."

Her voice is sharp, unwavering.

Ulisses blinks up at her through the haze of exhaustion.

"It took you three hours."

His stomach drops. Three hours?

Isabella's eyes are cold, unwavering. "As punishment, one hundred push-ups. One hundred pull-ups."

Ulisses stares at her, his arms already feeling like dead weight. His lungs are still struggling to pull in air. His mind protests, "I can't."

But he doesn't say it.

He swallows the doubt.

His hands press into the dirt, and the only words that leave his lips are

"Yes, Mother."

And he begins.

As Ulisses struggles through the final repetitions of his punishment, his arms shaking, his breath ragged, Helena approaches from the river, three freshly caught fish in hand. Water drips from their silvery scales as she hoists them up triumphantly.

"I got breakfast," she announces.

Isabella barely glances at her, her focus still on Ulisses as he pushes through the last of his pull-ups. Finally, as he finishes, collapsing onto his knees, Isabella takes the fish from Helena without a word and walks toward the fire she had prepared earlier.

Helena watches Ulisses for a moment before stepping toward him, pulling a small

William Henry Belmont

cloth from her pocket. His head is bowed, sweat dripping steadily from his face, creating dark patches in the dirt beneath him.

"Here," she says, offering the cloth. "Dry yourself."

Ulisses takes it without hesitation, dragging it across his forehead and then down the back of his neck. His muscles still throb from exhaustion, every fiber of his body aching.

With a small wave of her hand, Helena conjures a wooden cup filled with water, she bends slightly towards him and says, "Here. Take it."

Ulisses does not think twice. He surges forward, seizing the cup with both hands, and drinks it down in one gulp.

"Sit, Ulisses," Helena says gently.

She lowers herself onto the ground, crossing her legs in front of her, hands resting on her knees. Ulisses hesitates only for a moment before mimicking her posture.

"Breathe," she instructs. "Just breathe."

Ulisses inhales deeply, the crisp morning air filling his burning lungs. It feels like the first real breath he's taken in hours.

"Good," Helena says, her voice soothing. "Now, breathe in again. Slowly."

He does as she says, his chest expanding.

"And breathe out. Even slower."

Ulisses exhales, feeling some of the tension in his shoulders begin to ease.

"Close your eyes," Helena murmurs.

He hesitates but obeys. Darkness surrounds him.

"Meditation is not about silencing your mind," she continues. "It is about guiding it. Right now, your body is exhausted, and your thoughts are restless. You're thinking about the pain in your arms, the fire in your lungs, how much you want to rest."

Ulisses swallows. She's right.

"But your body is only part of who you are," Helena says. "Your mind and your will, they must be stronger than your flesh. That

William Henry Belmont

is how you will control the relics. That is how they will listen to you."

Ulisses listens intently, keeping his breathing steady.

"Feel the air as it enters your lungs, filling you," she continues. "Feel the weight of your body against the earth. Do not resist it. Let it ground you."

He does as she says, focusing on the sensation. His heart, once hammering, begins to slow into a steady rhythm.

"You must learn to focus yourself. To quiet the doubts, the fears, the distractions. Power is not just strength of the body, Ulisses, it is clarity of mind. It is focus. The relics are not weapons to be wielded. They are extensions of your will. If your mind is undisciplined, they will not respond."

Ulisses' brows furrow slightly, but he doesn't break his breathing rhythm.

"Now," Helena says, "I want you to picture something. The relics, yours and your mother's. See them in your mind. Feel their presence."

Ulisses does. In his mind, he sees the bracelet, pendant, and hair tie, glowing softly in the darkness.

"Now, reach for them, not with your hands, but with your mind. Will them to come to you."

Ulisses concentrates, feeling the strange pull of something deep inside him, something unfamiliar, yet not entirely foreign.

Helena's voice remains steady. "In time, this will become second nature. But for now, just breathe."

And so, Ulisses breathes, the world around him fading, his mind sharpening, reaching for something just beyond his grasp.

Helena and Ulisses continue to breathe in and out, their breaths synchronized with the tranquil rhythm of the Sanctuary of Echoes. The air here is unlike anything Ulisses has ever known, cool, crisp, and impossibly pure. With each inhale, his chest expands, filling with something more than just air. With each exhale, the tension in

William Henry Belmont

his body ebbs away, like waves retreating from the shore.

Slowly, his heartbeat steadies. The fire in his lungs fade away. His aching muscles, once stiff with exhaustion, feel lighter, looser. The world around him, once overwhelming, now feels distant, quiet, controlled.

After a few minutes, Helena's voice, soft but firm, breaks the silence.

"Breathe out... and open your eyes."

Ulisses exhales slowly, releasing the last remnants of fatigue, and then opens his eyes.

The world is unchanged, yet different. The river still flows; the grass still sways gently in the wind. But something within him has shifted.

He feels calm. At peace.

More than that, he feels strong.

His muscles, which had burned with exhaustion, no longer throb. His mind, which had been clouded with doubt, now feels clear. He looks down at his hands, flexing his fingers, as if testing the sensation of this newfound stillness.

Helena watches him closely, a small smile forming on her lips. "That is the power of the mind, Ulisses. Strength is not just in the body. You must master both."

Ulisses meets her gaze, realization dawning in his eyes. This was only the beginning. "Thank you, godmother." Ulisses says.

Both Helena and Ulisses stand up, their movements in sync as they walk back toward Isabella, who has finished preparing the food. The smell of freshly cooked fish fills the air, and Ulisses' stomach growls in anticipation. He and Helena sit down with Isabella, and the three of them begin to eat in silence, the crackling of the fire the only sound.

Ulisses glances at his mother, noting the softness in her expression that he hasn't seen since before the training began. She looks back at him, her eyes calm, filled with a love that has never wavered, even in the midst of everything. For a moment, they share a quiet, knowing smile, a simple gesture that speaks volumes, one of reassurance, understanding, and unspoken bonds. Then, with a deep breath, they return to their meal, the silence now more peaceful than before.

After they finish eating, they sit comfortably for a while, resting. Ulisses feels the weight of the day, the training, the strain of pushing his body beyond its limits. But for now, he lets himself relax, taking in the serenity of the place.

It's Isabella who breaks the silence first, standing up abruptly.

"Helena, can you help me here?" she asks, her voice carrying an undercurrent of determination.

Helena smiles, already knowing exactly what Isabella needs. With a wave of her hand, two wooden training dummies materialize out of thin air. They stand tall and solid, their shapes rough and basic, perfect for practicing.

Isabella walks toward one of the dummies, her gaze sharp and unwavering as she turns to Ulisses, who is just beginning to rise to his feet, still sore from his punishment.

"Come here. You're not done for the day," she says, her voice carrying a weight of finality. The intensity in her eyes returns, hardening like steel.

Ulisses, feeling the shift in the atmosphere, straightens up. The relaxed moment is gone, replaced by the familiar fire that burns in his mother's gaze. He swallows, nodding silently, and steps toward her.

"You've never fought in your life," Isabella continues, her voice brisk, instructing. "So, we're going to start slow."

She stands in front of him, demonstrating the form. She clenches her fist, bringing it back to her side, and then with a swift motion, she thrusts her fist forward, hitting the dummy with a sharp, practiced strike. "This is how you throw a punch," she says, her tone steady and precise.

William Henry Belmont

Ulisses watches closely, nodding, trying to absorb every detail. He raises his hand, mimicking her stance, unsure but determined. Isabella steps back, observing.

Ulisses throws his first punch, awkward but with the right intention. It connects with the dummy, but not with the power or precision she demonstrated. Isabella nods slightly, but it's clear that she expects more.

"Again," she orders, and she demonstrates once again.

This time, Ulisses focuses harder, tightening his form. He punches again, with more speed, more focus.

Isabella watches him closely, then steps forward. "Good. Now a quick upper cut after your punch." She shows him the technique, her foot work, like a one-two combination.

Ulisses follows her instructions, practicing again and again. His body feels sore, but his mind is sharper. Every movement, every technique is an opportunity to learn, an opportunity to prove himself.

"Combination," Isabella instructs next. "Jab, cross, hook. Like this." She demonstrates again, fluid in her movements, her punches quick and precise.

Ulisses practices, his arms growing heavy with each repetition, sweat dripping down his face. The movements begin to feel natural, his rhythm building slowly.

"Again," Isabella says, as she steps away and joins Helena by the fire.

Ulisses does not hesitate. He continues, repeating the combinations until the sun dips lower in the sky, the light turning golden and then orange. His muscles ache, his breath ragged, but he keeps going. Each punch, each strike becomes sharper, more controlled. There's no room for doubt now. He's past the point of questioning whether he can do it or not. This is the beginning of something new, something hard, but necessary.

And as he continues his practice, Isabella and Helena stand to the side, watching him in silence. There's no need for

further words. This is the way forward, and
Ulisses is beginning to understand it.

Ulisses opens his eyes, his heart
racing with anticipation. The morning air
feels crisp, full of possibility; he jumps
up with a burst of energy, his body already
aching with anticipation. He stretches his
arms and legs, feeling the tightness in his
muscles as they respond to the morning
routine. He throws a few punches and kicks,
the rhythm of his movements flowing smoothly
as he warms up. Each motion feels more
natural than the last, his form improving
every day.

With his body now primed, he takes off
toward the tree in the distance. His pace
is steady, his breath controlled, and his
legs carry him forward effortlessly. The
tree, once a daunting target, now seems
closer with each stride. He reaches it and
touches the rough bark, the cool sensation
grounding him before he spins around and
begins his run back. His feet hit the earth
with purpose, his body lighter than it has

ever felt. The rhythmic pounding of his steps echoes in his mind, keeping him focused.

When he finally returns to the camp, he notices that his mother and godmother are already by the fire, preparing breakfast. The smell of food mixes with the fresh air, making his stomach growl. As he walks toward the river, he smiles at his mother. His mother's gaze meets his, calm, steady, and proud.

"Good job, son," Isabella calls out from across the camp, her voice carrying the familiar tone of approval. "Just under 55 minutes."

Ulisses nods, his muscles burning from the exertion, but a sense of accomplishment fills him. As he sits down by the river to catch his breath, he can't help but feel a rush of gratitude for this moment. He closes his eyes, the world around him fading as he shifts into the peaceful space that meditation brings. The sound of the river flowing, the rustle of the trees in the gentle breeze, all of it becomes background noise as he focuses himself.

Helena, standing nearby, watches him for a moment before turning to Isabella with a soft smile.

"These last two years have been great for him," Helena says, her voice warm with pride.

Isabella nods, her eyes following Ulisses as he settles into his meditation. "Yes, he's getting better so fast," she agrees, her smile matching Helena's.

The two women share a knowing glance, the kind that comes from seeing their efforts come to fruition. It's a quiet moment of shared pride, one that speaks of the long road they've traveled and the journey still ahead.

Ulisses, eyes closed, begins to find his peace. The past two years of grueling training, sweat, pain, and sacrifices. But at this moment, all he has to do is breathe, focus, and trust that he is becoming who he was always meant to be.

Once Ulisses finishes his morning meditation, he opens his eyes to the golden light of the dawn stretching across the Sanctuary. The cool morning breeze brushes against his face, carrying the scent of the river and the fire where breakfast is being prepared. He takes one last deep breath before rising to his feet. His body no longer aches the way it once did; the training has strengthened him beyond recognition.

He walks toward his mother and godmother, who are already seated by the fire. Isabella, tending to the last of the fish, looks up as he approaches.

He sits down beside them, reaching for his portion as they begin to eat. The warmth of the meal settles in him, and for a moment, they sit in comfortable silence, appreciating the simple pleasure of food shared among family.

After a few bites, Isabella looks at him, her expression softening. "You've come so far, Ulisses," she says, her voice carrying both warmth and pride. "Two years

William Henry Belmont

ago, you were barely able to lift my axe without stumbling. Now, you wield it as if it's an extension of yourself."

Ulisses lowers his gaze slightly, not out of shyness, but because hearing his mother's praise is something precious. He has spent so long trying to prove himself, and now, here she was, acknowledging what he has become.

She continues, "And it's not just the axe, you've mastered the other two relics as well. The way you call upon their power, the way you adapt… You're no longer just learning. You're becoming."

Ulisses swallows, nodding once. He won't let the words go to his head, but he will carry them with him.

Then Helena speaks, her voice gentle yet firm. "That's all good, but strength is more than just what your body can do," she says, watching him carefully. "And it's more than just discipline or focus. True strength, Ulisses, comes from here." She places a hand over his heart.

Ulisses looks at her, listening closely.

"You can be the fastest, the strongest, the smartest fighter in the world, but if your heart isn't in it, if you don't understand why you fight, then all of it is meaningless," she continues. "Strength without purpose is just violence."

Ulisses nods again, slower this time. He understands.

He fights for the people who had sacrificed for him. For the legacy he carries. For those who could not fight for themselves.

Helena watches him, her green eyes full of wisdom. "Well, let's continue training" she says. "We need to keep practicing your mastery of the three relics, used together as if they were one."

As they finish their meal and begin to rise, a heavy stillness settles over the Sanctuary of Echoes, an unnatural silence that presses against their senses.

William Henry Belmont

Then, from the distance, a figure
emerges.

Isabella's breath catches in her
throat. A cold weight settles in her chest
as she recognizes the shadowy figure
approaching them. Her heart drops.

A slow, taunting clap echoes through
the space.

"Well, here you are," says the familiar
voice, smooth, laced with amusement.

Ulisses turns sharply, his muscles
tensing. Helena's expression hardens; her
sharp gaze locked onto the intruder. But
beneath her composure, her mind races. *How
is this possible?*

Luca steps forward, his dark cloak
shifting like a living shadow around him.
His smirk is infuriatingly confident, his
blue eyes studying the sanctuary and our
heroes.

"You didn't really think you could hide
from me forever, did you?" he asks, tilting
his head slightly. His voice is casual, but
there's an unmistakable weight behind it,
like a predator toying with its prey.

Isabella instinctively moves in front of Ulisses, her stance protective. Helena shifts beside her, ready for whatever comes next.

Luca chuckles, the sound low and mocking.

"You know," he says, his fingers tightening around something in his hand, "this place was hard to find." He then looks directly to Helena, "but not impossible, I also have two relics, remember."

With a slow, deliberate motion, he lifts his hand, revealing the worn, ancient tome. Merlin's Tome. Then Luca lifts his other hand slightly, almost as a taunt, drawing their attention to his finger. A black ring gleams in the light, a dark aura pulsing around it. Morgana's Ring.

A smirk forms on Luca's lips as he watches the realization dawn on their faces.

His eyes flicker toward Ulisses, amusement dancing in them. "Did you really think I'd let you be the only one to grow stronger?"

William Henry Belmont

Isabella's hands curl into fists. Helena's lips press into a thin line. Ulisses steps forward, muscles tensed, mind clear, heart ready.

Luca laughs, the sound sharp, cutting through the thick tension.

"This," he says, lifting the tome slightly, and transforming the ring into Morgana's staff "is going to be fun."

Part 9: One Last Hope

William Henry Belmont

Luca and Ulisses stand face to face in the vast, open veldt, the wind carrying the scent of grass and the distant hum of an impending storm. The sky, once a serene blue, seemed to darken as the two warriors locked eyes.

"Ah, ah, ah... do you really think a few years of playing warrior will make you my equal?" Luca mused, his voice carrying both amusement and menace. His piercing gaze glanced toward Isabella and Helena, who stood at a safe distance, watching with tense anticipation. "You know this changes nothing. No matter how many relics you wield, fate will remain the same."

Ulisses didn't flinch. He brought his hands together, and in an instant, the enchanted hair tie unraveled, its golden threads expanding into a radiant suit of armor that wrapped around him, shimmering with an otherworldly glow. The bracelet on his wrist pulsed with energy before morphing into a silver shield, its surface gleaming like moonlight on water. Finally, his mother's pendant trembled before erupting into its true form, Sir Percival's mighty axe, its polished blade humming with untold earthen power.

"It ends today," Ulisses declared, his voice steady, unwavering.

Luca smirked, his lips curling into a dark grin. "Ah, ah, ah. I heard that before"

Then, without warning, Ulisses surged forward, faster than the wind. He swung the axe in a wide arc, its blade cutting through the air with a low, resonant hum. Luca sidestepped the first strike with effortless grace, then another, his movements fluid like a shadow dancing between candle flames. But Ulisses was relentless. He pressed on, his strikes coming faster, each one heavier than the last. Sparks flew as the axe clashed against an powerful barrier of dark energy conjured by Luca's outstretched hand.

"You have spirit," Luca chuckled, dodging another sweeping blow, "but spirit alone is not enough."

With a flick of his wrist, Luca unleashed a surge of dark magic, a spiraling

William Henry Belmont

vortex of black flames that roared toward Ulisses. Instinctively, Ulisses raised his shield, the silver surface absorbing the attack, but the force still sent him skidding back. Before he could recover, Luca lunged, his hand crackling with obsidian lightning. He struck, aiming for Ulisses' chest, but Ulisses twisted, parrying the blow with the flat of his axe before countering with a diagonal slash.

For a moment, they were evenly matched. Ulisses weaving through Luca's onslaught of dark tendrils and shadow-infused strikes, Luca deftly dodging the axe's devastating arcs. Blades of wind and earth erupted from their clashes, tearing the grass from the earth beneath them.

Then Luca laughed.

In a blur of motion Ulisses swung, but the moment his attack missed, Luca's fist crashed into his ribs like a hammer, sending him tumbling across the veldt. Ulisses barely had time to recover before Luca extended his hand, summoning a torrent of shadowy chains that lashed out like serpents. Ulisses raised his shield, but the impact was immense, the dark tendrils wrapping around him, constricting.

"Did you really think you could win?" Luca taunted, his voice laced with mockery.

From afar, Isabella's eyes widened. She could see it, the moment her son would fall, just as his father had. But she would not allow it.

She clasped her hands together, whispering an incantation in a language older than time itself. The air around her shimmered, her life force pouring into the spell. A golden aura erupted from her, spreading across the battlefield like a tidal wave of light. It wrapped around Ulisses, filling him with warmth, with love, his mother's final gift. Isabella had given his life to her son, to give him a chance to win.

Ulisses gasped as the power surged through him. His wounds closed, his strength multiplied, and his mind became clearer than ever before. The aura around him burned like a star, forcing Luca to take a step back.

William Henry Belmont

Ulisses lifted his axe, his voice steady, filled with resolve. "This is for my mother. For my father."

He launched forward, his movements now beyond human. His axe carved through the air with the force of a tempest, each strike faster and sharper than before. Luca barely managed to evade them, his smirk finally faltering.

Ulisses struck again. And again. Each blow came closer, the force of the attacks pushing Luca back. The ground beneath them cracked. The air trembled. Luca's expression hardened. He had underestimated him.

And then,

"AHHH" Ulisses roared.

His armor shimmered, brighter than it ever had before, his shield hardening until it gleamed like pure moonlight. Something within him shifted. From his right hand poured a power he had never been able to summon before, magic that carried both fire and light, fierce and unyielding. He pressed his glowing palm against the blade of his axe, and Percival's weapon answered.

Echoes of Legends

The steel transformed.

The blade burned with a new radiance, no longer merely forged, but awakened, a weapon meant to erase darkness itself.

Ulisses brought the axe down in a mighty arc.

For the first time, fear crossed Luca's face.

The strike landed true, cleaving through Luca's shoulder and cutting cleanly through his chest. Ulisses stood face to face with him, his expression of a son avenging his mother, his father, and a broken world. Luca's strength weakened. His breath left him. His body fell still.

Peace washed over Ulisses, and Helena, smiling from afar. A fragile serenity born from believing, at last, that it was over.

"Helena," Ulisses said, looking at his godmother, "we did it… we won"

Helena formed a small smile, tears of joy almost falling from her eyes. She could not believe that, after all these years, all that training, all the sacrifice. Finally, the world would be a better place. The war

William Henry Belmont

that started ages ago with King Arthur and his court against Morgana La Fey was finally over.

"Ah… ah… ah."

The sound came from directly in front of Ulisses.

Ulisses' breath caught.

Before he could understand how, Luca stood there, whole, untouched. With a lazy gesture, Luca waved his hand. The lifeless body impaled by Percival's axe faded away, dissolving into nothingness from the cruel illusion it was.

Luca's eyes locked onto Ulisses.

"Power and resources will always triumph over righteousness, boy."

The words struck harder than any blade.

Ulisses froze, the truth crashing into him too late. Luca extended his hand, darkness coiling eagerly around it. A lance of pure darken flame formed in an instant, and Luca hurled it forward.

The strike hit its mark with merciless precision. Ulisses took his last breath while Luca's dark-energy lance pierced his chest.

Hope shattered.

Arthur's court fell with it.

From afar, Helena sighed.

The battlefield was eerily silent. The sounds of battle had faded, leaving only the whisper of the wind and the weight of defeat hanging in the air. The lifeless body of Ulisses fell right next to Luca.

Helena stood, her body trembling, eyes fixed on the wreckage of what was left of the fight. Her hands, stained with the blood of those who had followed her, hung limply at her sides. Her breath came in short gasps, the weight of the loss settling deeper with every passing second.

Luca approached her, his steps quiet, but purposeful. His eyes met hers, cold and unfeeling. A bitter, almost amused smirk tugged at the corner of his mouth as he regarded her.

"Were you expecting any other ending?" he said, his voice barely more than a whisper, but it carried the heaviness of inevitability.

He took a step closer, his gaze never leaving hers. "None of it matter. Your lineage, your blood, your training, your desires... none of it did. It was always going to end this way."

Luca's words were final, and they sliced through the air like a blade. "It ended with what it would have always had... with me winning."

Helena's heart sank at his words. She wanted to scream, to lash out, but there was no strength left. Only the crushing realization that everything, the hope, the sacrifice, the pain, had been for nothing. Tears flooded her eyes, one after another, slipping down her cheeks.

She closed her eyes and took a deep breath, her chest tightening with the weight of it all. Her body dropped as the truth took hold, a truth that she had fought so desperately to avoid.

The faces of the fallen flashed before her eyes, those who had believed in her, who had trusted in the dream she had sold them. And now they were all gone. For what?

Nothing.

She fell to her knees, her tears falling freely now. The quiet surrounding them felt unbearable, like the world had forgotten to mourn the loss of so much.

Luca stood above her, looking down with disdain, a figure of triumph against the backdrop of utter desolation. "Do not worry, Helena Emeris," he said, "you will live, only to be torture by your defeat and what you costed others."

And then, through the hollow silence, Helena screams at the top of her lungs, "Merlin... you told that if I..." But she stops, there was nobody left to hear her, so she whispers to herself, barely audible through her sobs: *What have I done..."*

William Henry Belmont

Epilogue

Several years had passed since the great battle between Ulisses and Luca. The world, as it always did, moved on. The streets busy with merchants calling out their wares, children playing in the dirt, and farmers tended their fields. There were no grand celebrations, no monuments raised for the fallen. For the common folk, rulers came and went, banners changed color, and yet the rhythm of daily life remained the same.

Helena's name became a whisper. Her rebellion, her dream, faded into the past, remembered only in hushed voices by those who still dared to believe in something more. The heroes who had once stood tall, their sacrifices, their hopes, all seemed to vanish like footprints in the sand.

And yet, the world was not entirely unchanged. The mentor, now a wanderer in the land she had fought to protect, saw it in the eyes of those who had been there. A quiet resolve, a lingering question, a flicker of something that had not been there before. The seeds of defiance, of choice, of understanding. Perhaps not today, perhaps not tomorrow, but one day, someone would remember.

She disappeared into the shadows, feeling defeated, but knowing that even if history turned to dust, the struggle had not been in vain. The battle may have been lost, but battles were never the whole war.

And though Luca ruled, draped in the weight of his victory, he too must have known, his power will never be eternal.

For now, people went about their lives, eyes lowered, hands busy. But somewhere, someday, someone would dare to look up.

After the Story, To the Reader

William Henry Belmont

If you have made it this far, allow me to thank you for staying.

What you have just read was never meant to be only a written story. It was written as a foundation, for people of greater skills than my own to sketch a world from words. A world waiting to be questioned, challenged, and tested.

At its heart, it imagines four heroes drawn together to contain a power greater than any one of them alone. What they are willing to risk, or indeed do, is not fixed.

Would you train them longer before facing the final battle? Would you press forward, knowing they are not physically prepared, trusting instead in strategy? Would you accept sacrifice if it meant the end was within your reach?

I wanted this story to feel as though there was always a little more to be told, not because it was missing, but because it was waiting.

Every choice, every silence, every conflict was placed not to conclude a tale, but to invite more.

The kinds of stories that shaped my imagination were always those of a world in peril, a group of four heroes standing to save it, and the uneasy truth that victory is never free.

What remains is what *you* would ask of those four heroes… and of yourself.

William Henry Belmont